Murder by Adjudication

By Debra K. Dunlap

To Jessica Loeper, for support, encouragement and commas.

To Heather Haven, for inspiration and kindness.

Cover art by

Copper Owl
{PRESS}

www.copperowlpress.com

Who watches the watchmen?

Attributed to the Roman poet Juvenal from his *Satires*

Chapter One

It all began when I fell onto the dead body.

Yes, I said fell *onto* the dead body. Face to face. Cheek to cheek. Much too up close and personal for comfort. I stayed because I could hear the killer ransacking the county attorney's office next door. Silently thanking the dead guy for muffling the sound of my clumsy fall, I lay in the same position for what felt like hours.

Finally, the click of a light switch echoed in the empty hall, followed by the faint sound of footsteps muffled in the heavy carpet outside my office. Afraid to turn my head, I saw only the dim glow of a tiny flashlight beam in my peripheral vision.

The urge to run warred with the instinct to hide and so I did neither. I froze in place, squeezing my eyes shut and embracing the dead man as if he were my savior. The scent of his aftershave filled my nostrils and his five o'clock shadow scratched my cheek.

I nearly cried out when I heard the heavy breathing at the door. It sounded like the killer had worn himself out with the exertion of destroying the neighboring office. I figured he'd start on mine next and find me, but instead he closed the door.

Trying not to think about the unknown and unmoving man beneath me, I stayed where I'd fallen until I heard the roar of a car engine in the parking lot. When I felt sure the mystery man had

1

gone, I crept across the dark room, fumbled for the telephone on my desk and dialed 911.

****

"Okay, explain why you were in the courthouse at this late hour." Jim Robinson, a handsome Deputy Sheriff, focused his blue eyes on my face. "Sorry, Indie, but you know I have to ask these questions. Hang on." He scratched his pen on the edge of the paper in his clipboard. "Alright, now it's working. Go ahead."

"Yes, I know you have to ask. I needed my violin. I left it here earlier this evening." I jerked my head toward the corner of the room where I'd parked the battered case. "Right over there. I came to get it so I could practice before bed."

"Why did you leave the case here?"

"I played in the concert in the park tonight with the rest of my band." I knew he'd seen me there. He'd been in the audience. "We all went to dinner afterward and I left the violin here so I wouldn't have to take it into Hiroto's Restaurant. You know how crowded that place is."

Jim tapped his pen on the clipboard. "Why didn't the rest of your band leave their instruments here?"

"They all drove to the concert, so they put their stuff in the trunk. I walked. You know I live just a couple of blocks from here and Hiroto's is right around the corner."

"Why didn't you ride with someone else or drive your car?"

"Because I like to walk." After spending part of the night perched atop a dead man, my nerves were shot and the questions began to rankle.

"Fine. You played your violin in the park and then left it in the office. You went to dinner at Hiroto's and then returned to pick up the violin about what time?"

"Between eleven and eleven-thirty, after we peeled Gerry off the barstool. He's like that since Laverne left him." The aforementioned Gerry Marner, who played upright bass in our bluegrass band, had milked the poor-me-my-wife-left-me routine for over a year. He tried my patience at the best of times.

I continued, "Anyway, I came down the hall in the dark and couldn't find my keys. I noticed the office door slightly ajar and walked inside, but only made it a few steps before I tripped."

"That's when you fell on the deceased?"

I glared at Jim. "I know you're a rookie and like to show off the lingo, but you know Winston Oligite's name as well as I do. He was a nice man and deserves better than 'deceased.'"

A fetching blush crept from under Jim's shirt collar and progressed up his neck to land with an explosion of red on his cheeks.

"Sorry, Indie. You're right."

A sigh of regret escaped from between my lips as I restrained myself from running a hand through his magnificent dark hair. Too young, too eager, too needy. Besides, I have a hunk boyfriend. "No problem. I guess I'm a bit jumpy, too. Don't see too many dead people in my line of work."

I work as a private investigator, mostly divorce stuff and employment screening with occasional odd jobs for local attorneys. My little office, home away from home for three years, stands in the basement of the courthouse. The county graciously allows me to pay twice as much rent as the office space is worth, but the location is golden for drop-in business.

Jim gave me a nervous grin. "Let's finish up so you can go home."

"Not much else to tell. I heard crashing and banging in the next office, so I stayed put. A guy came out of the office breathing as if he'd just finished the Boston Marathon, stopped for a minute to close my door and then left. I didn't see him."

"If you didn't see him, how do you know it was a guy and not a woman?"

"There was something about the footsteps. I couldn't hear them well because of the carpet, but the sound, the pacing, was wrong for a woman."

"Any idea what Mr. Oligite was doing in your office at night?"

"Nope. No idea." I shook my head and reached to push my glasses further up on my face. No glasses.

"I think that's it for now, although there may be more questions later." Handsome Jim stuck his pen in his pocket and tucked the clipboard under his arm before giving me a friendly pat on the shoulder. "Go home and get some rest."

"What about my office? Can I go in yet?" Thankfully, the coroner and his men had removed Winston Oligite's body. From the bench where I sat across from the slightly ajar door, I could see several deputies still dusting for fingerprints.

"It may be awhile yet. Why don't you go home and come back in the morning?"

"No, I want to see if anything is missing. Isn't that something you'll need to know?"

An arm grabbed me from behind and jerked me off the bench into a smothering embrace. "Darling, are you alright? Why didn't you call me?"

Despite the genuine concern in his voice, the faint odor of beer on his breath irritated me. "Let go of me. I'm fine. I didn't call because I've been busy." I shoved against his chest to free myself and took a step backward.

Peter Hampton, my knockdown gorgeous, on-again, off-again boyfriend of three years stood before me. In the middle of the night, despite his obvious genuine worry for me, he'd taken time to comb his thick, black hair and change out of his deputy sheriff uniform into jeans (nothing wrong with the rear view on this guy) and a green button-up shirt.

I sighed again.

"Hey, Pete. How goes it?" Jim's face held a careful, neutral expression.

"Fine, buddy. Just fine. Thanks for taking care of my girl."
He held a hand out to the other deputy.

"Just doing my job."

Peter smoothed his hair and returned his attention to me.
"Indie, darling, are you sure you're okay? You look a bit peaked.
This must have been a terrible ordeal for you."

"I told you I'm fine. I'm tired and I need a cup of coffee." I
peered through the door and pointed at the machine sitting on a
table by my desk. "Jim, I don't suppose you'd let me make myself
a cup."

"Sorry, but no."

"A cup of coffee is the last thing you need. Let's go home
and I'll make a nice cup of tea for you." Peter put his arm around
my shoulder.

"Would you mind grabbing my glasses for me, Jim? They
went flying across the carpet when I fell." I tugged Peter's arm,
drawing him away from Jim and the open door to my office.
"Home? I'm going home *alone* as soon as I get my glasses. I
appreciate your concern, but please stop treating me as if I were a
child. There's not a thing wrong with me other than a lack of sleep.
I'll happily accept a ride if you care to offer one or I can call a cab
if you have something else to do."

Peter sulked the two blocks to my house, as I'd known he
would. I looked at him sideways, unable to resist his Hollywood
good looks, but trying to avoid eye contact. Any perceived sign of
weakness on my part tended to serve as a catalyst for a spate of

temper. His movie star appearance brought him plenty of female adulation besides mine, which tended to wax and wane. Oddly enough, we'd been mistaken several times for brother and sister. Not because I'm as gorgeous as he is, but because we share the same black hair, bright green eyes and high cheekbones. I'm twenty-nine, a year younger than Peter.

I pushed my glasses in place (why do they never fit right?) and jumped out of the car. "I'll call you tomorrow. Thanks for the ride."

I slammed the door shut and he drove off without answering. Despite the show of bravado for Peter, my heart pounded as I opened the door and reached around the doorjamb to flick the light switch on before slipping inside. My tension dissolved at the sight of my intact home and I gained an added sense of security after locking doors and windows.

After brewing a cup of coffee, I settled in a chair with a book and propped my feet on the footstool. If the night's devastation had extended to my little home, I'd have screamed loud enough to wake people in the next county. I loved the simple, un-fussy house; the living room walls lined with overflowing bookshelves, plain linen curtains, chocolate-brown leather sofa and chair, several music stands, the bright red geranium given to me by the Oligites as a thank you gift after I'd dug up information proving their son hadn't vandalized the local flower shop.

The Oligites...what a shame about Winston Oligite. His wife, Sylvia seemed truly fond of him. Their son, Robert, proved as clean as a whistle when I'd checked him out at Winston's insistence several months ago. "I *know* my son, Miss Stevens. Kids these days are wild, too self-centered. Sylvia and me, we've been careful to watch over our boy so he wouldn't do those things. We want him to grow up right."

I listened to him plead and shook my head, feeling sorry for him. "Winston, you've known me long enough to call me by my first name. Well, my nickname...Indie."

His forehead creased. "Indie is such an odd name."

I rolled my eyes. "I know, but it's better than Indianetta."

"Indianetta?"

"Yes, my mother had a thing for some movie star and the name is from one of his movies. Now, Winston, I hate to say this, but half a dozen witnesses saw your son break into that shop."

"They're lying, Miss Stevens, uh, Indie. I tell you, our Robert did not do this."

In the end, I'd agreed to help him, to investigate his son, despite the unorthodoxy of the job and my doubts regarding the outcome. However, after some digging and interviewing I came to believe in Robert's innocence. I organized the evidence I'd gathered and gave it to Winston to present to Robert's attorney.

Something odd about that whole juvie case. After I tracked down the out-of-town tutor who affirmed Robert's attendance at a math session during the time of the break-in, the witnesses melted away. Even stranger, the entire juvenile case file disappeared from the courthouse records to the dismay and horror of Clara

Hofstedder, the elderly and unimaginative Clerk of Court. Curious and curiouser.

I didn't notice slipping into a doze until something startled me awake. It took a moment for my eyes to focus, but I'd have sworn I saw the doorknob turn. Just slightly, as if someone wanted to test the lock. Shaking off my imagination-fuelled jumpiness, I dragged myself from the chair, turned off the lights and went to bed.

The next morning a Beethoven ringtone blasted me awake. Barely. I fumbled for my cell phone without lifting my head. "Yes?"

"Indie, is that you? I've called half a dozen times." Ruby Langdon, my best friend and favorite attorney, sounded worried.

"Mm, yes, it's me."

"Are you sure you're okay? You don't sound good."

I rolled onto my back with a groan. "Fine, just exhausted. I spent most of the night answering questions."

"Yes, I heard about Winston's murder. Unbelievable. And just when the Oligites' lives were getting back to normal after the debacle with their son."

Suppressing a yawn, I maneuvered myself into a sitting position and slid my feet into slippers. "Can I call you back in a few? I need a cup of coffee and a shower."

"How about if I buy you lunch? You take your shower and I'll pick you up in half an hour. I want to hear about last night."

I lost the battle with the yawn. "Okay, sounds good. See you in thirty."

The shower revived me somewhat, the coffee a bit more. I opened the curtains, unlocked the front door and then returned to the kitchen to wait while my coffee maker brewed a second cup.

The door opened and Ruby hollered. "Where are you? Indie, are you ready?"

"In the kitchen. Come on in."

As elegant as usual, Ruby's dark green suit brought an air of holiday festivity to my red-and-white checked kitchen décor. She's one of those women who manage to make everything look easy, from getting a juris doctorate at Columbia University to running a household that includes two children. Her husband Mark, a computer genius, worships her.

"Let's go. You can tell me about last night on the way to the Sandwich Shoppe. I've got court this afternoon and I'm starving."

Gulping my second cup, I snatched my purse from the counter and followed Ruby to the front door, listening to the story of the latest accomplishments of her adorable children.

"We knew he reads above his grade level, but would you believe it? He checked out a book called *Fallon O'Reilly & the Ice Queen's Lair* and read it in one night! The school librarian is astounded...oopf. Indie, what is it? Is something wrong?"

I hardly noticed Ruby banging into my back when I stopped right outside the door. The hair on my arms stood straight up and a metallic taste filled my mouth.

Footprints. Footprints under the windows above my flowerbeds. Muddy footprints leading straight to my front door.

Chapter Two

My hands continued to shake as Ruby drove across town to the Sandwich Shoppe and parked. We found a seat in a booth flanked by red vinyl-covered benches and waited for our cream of broccoli soup and turkey sandwiches on fresh-baked, whole wheat bread.

"I was so sleep-fuzzy that I assumed it was my imagination, thinking the door knob rattled. You know, part of a dream or something. Besides, I still felt a little shook up over falling on a dead guy."

Ruby shook her shiny, red hair and reached across the table to tap my forearm. "My God, of course you were shook up. You must have been terrified. How often does such a thing happen?"

Not often around here because our quiet, little town seldom saw more than one serious violation of the law every decade or two. Thank God. "I was too busy trying to keep quiet to be scared while the office next door was ransacked. By the time I got home and thought I heard the door knob rattling, I was too sleepy to care what was going on."

"I don't like this." Ruby frowned. "I would say it was your bad luck to have a peeping tom outside your window, except it doesn't strike me as coincidental. Too many things happening in one night. Did you call the police?"

"About the noise outside? No, I thought it was probably me being jumpy. I mean, hey, it's not every day my clumsiness leads to falling on a…"

"Yeah, I know, falling on a dead guy. Listen, Indie, quit joking. I don't think you should treat this lightly. Jim Robinson is right over there having lunch with the Judge. Let's go talk to them."

"I'm not exactly dressed for judicial consultations, you know." I gestured toward my jeans and white blouse, my hair haphazardly constrained by two clips in the back.

"Oh, for crying out loud. We're not going into court." Ruby heaved a long-suffering sigh and dragged me over to the Judge's table. "Good afternoon, Your Honor. Indie needs to speak with Jim."

"Hello, Ms. Langdon. Yes, Ms. Stevens, I read an article in this morning's paper about the incident in the courthouse last night. Most unfortunate. Both of you please join us." Judge Beecher T. Oldham wiped his mouth with a delicate touch and laid the napkin beside his plate. "A most unsettling occurrence. How fortunate that the killer did not learn of your presence, Ms. Stevens. And you had further trouble or did you remember something you forgot to tell our good deputy?"

Constituents loved Judge Oldham. They voted to retain him by a huge majority at the end of every judicial term. He kissed babies, talked shooting or fishing with male voters and helped elderly women cross the street. Every summer he invited county

14

residents to a Fourth of July barbecue at his ancestral home, a stately mansion on a hill overlooking the river. He looked almost a twin of the previous Judge, his now-deceased father. Tall, handsome, white-haired and blue-eyed. All-American.

I didn't like him.

"Well? Was there something you forgot to tell the deputy, Ms. Stevens?" Judge Oldham tugged at his shirt cuffs, aligning them evenly with the sleeves of his tailored jacket.

"Excuse me, Your Honor, but I think Indie needs to speak to Jim in private in the event the case comes before you." Ruby eyed the Judge.

"Of course, Ms. Langdon. I was just leaving." The Judge stood and placed several bills on the table. "Here, this should cover everyone's lunch. You'll take care of it, Jim? Thank you. I have several files to review before court this afternoon."

We thanked him and Ruby flashed one of her brilliant smiles. "See you in court, Your Honor."

"Something else happen?" Jim turned his head from me to Ruby.

"Someone tried to get into Indie's house last night. At least, someone turned the door knob and this morning we saw footprints in her flower bed." Ruby peered over her cup of coffee to look at Jim.

He turned to me. "Someone tried to get in your house last night? After the murder?"

At my nod, Jim stood. "Let me take care of the lunch bill and then we'll go take a look at those footprints."

"Indie, I've got to meet my client before our hearing, so I'll see you later, okay? Will you be in your office?" Ruby slung her expensive, leather purse over her shoulder.

"Yep. I'll catch a ride with Jim to the house and then walk to the courthouse."

Jim returned from the cash register, tucking his wallet into his back pocket. "I have to drop off some paperwork at the Clerk of Court office, so I can give you a ride to your office when we finish with the footprints."

The drive to my house took only moments. I clambered out of the patrol car and led the way. "The prints are right by the front door and in the flower bed under the living room window. Right here. I...I...."

"Where? I don't see anything." Jim squatted to peer closely at my front step.

"They're gone." Goosebumps erupted on my arms and I shivered. "I swear they were right here."

"Hey, it's okay. You were probably upset by the time you got home last night. It's no big deal, Indie."

"Those footprints weren't imaginary. Ask Ruby. She saw them, too." Finding the prints gone was somehow more frightening than seeing them. "Something or someone has wiped them away."

Jim gave me a sympathetic look. "Come on, let's go. I have docs to give the Clerk and I'm sure you want to check your office for missing items."

****

Obviously, the killer had visited my office first. It was a train wreck, a disaster of monumental proportions. Either a monstrously spoiled child suffered a violent tantrum or someone set a madman free to wreak his psychotic vengeance against the world using my office as a surrogate target. Drawers pulled out and contents smashed on the carpet. Locked file cabinets crowbarred open, the files ripped and tossed aside. My laptop a heap of plastic bits and circuit board shards. An expensive leather chair, an office-warming gift from my mother, dangled from a hole in the wall. A hole created by the nut, I might add. I felt like wailing in my grief and sense of violation.

Instead, I lit a forbidden cigarette and perched on the only undamaged item in the room, my desk. My grandfather, a renowned attorney, left the gigantic McDowell & Craig desk to me in his will, along with an office lease in perpetuity. Seems back in the day he'd made a large donation to keep the county out of a financial jam incurred when a deputy clerk disappeared after embezzling a huge sum of money. His only condition had been a lifetime office lease with the right to will the "honor" to his chosen descendant. Always a fair man, he insisted he pay reasonable rent, so the county truly profited by the arrangement. I figured I profited too…how many private investigators finagle a courthouse office?

I gave the behemoth, wood desk an idle pat. How wonderful it would be to have Grandfather here right now. His sage advice, keen sense of humor. White hair, blue eyes sparkling with wit. I love my parents dearly, but I was closer to Grandfather than anyone else. The familiar sense of loss made my chest ache.

Enough reminiscing. Time for a plan. How does one decide where to start cleaning a mess of such proportions? Do you begin at the edge and work your to the center? Or do you first remove large debris and then small? I slid off the desk and climbed the stairs to the first floor in search of the building maintenance and supply man. Wherever you start, it takes big trash bags.

As I reached the top step, a group of women huddled in the rotunda, whispering.

"Serves her right. She's so uppity, thinks she's smarter than everyone else." The vindictive expression on Rhoda Bellinger's face made the hair on my arms stand up. "And that ridiculous way she pokes those clip things in her hair, like she's too lazy to have it styled."

"Ssh." Someone jabbed an elbow into her ribs.

She whirled to face me and curled her lip before turning back to her friends. In a lower voice still loud enough to carry, she said, "I don't care. I can't stand the woman."

I shared the sentiment. The woman drove me crazy, spending working hours traveling from office to office, spreading poisonous, spiteful gossip. She lived for it, reveled in it. As little time as she spent at her desk in the Treasurer's office, she'd managed to keep her job for over thirty-five years. She was sixty-eight, looked ninety-five and behaved like an adolescent girl. I avoided her whenever possible.

Ignoring Rhoda's remarks, I smiled at the other women and cadged a roll of trash bags from the maintenance man.

"Me and Tom took a peek in your office this morning." Rufus Garrett, the short and burly head of maintenance, gave me a sympathetic look. "We'll give you a hand later this afternoon if we have time. Got a plugged sink upstairs we gotta fix first. If you want, you can stack the bags against the wall outside your door and we'll haul 'em out for you."

I decided to begin with the destroyed case files because I'd need to replace them. As I stuffed unreadable paper shreds into the trash bag, I jotted down case numbers on a notepad I'd begged from the county attorney's secretary. A pattern soon emerged. The intruder had systematically destroyed every document relating to juveniles; the research I'd conducted on behalf of attorneys, divorce cases with children involved, miscellaneous files with results of investigations involving children, such as that I'd done for Winston Oligite.

Ruby wandered in as I filled the tenth bag. "I can't stay. Mark called. He's working late, some computer emergency in one of the Judge's offices, so I've got to pick up the kids."

"That's okay. I'm ready to go home. I need sleep."

"Of course you do. You look exhausted."

"Gee, thanks." I grinned at her discomfiture. "Only teasing. I know I look a wreck. I didn't even comb my hair, just stuck it in the clips. I need a cup of coffee and some reading time, but I have a problem."

She frowned as she listened to my description of the missing files. "Another coincidence or not? Listen, I'll call in a few favors to attorney and secretary friends, get as many replacement documents as possible and I'll send copies of everything I have."

"Thanks. I especially need the Brodan file since it's up for review." The Court had sent Cindy Brodan, a fifteen-year old delinquent, to a juvenile home in Pennsylvania.

The state Juvenile Justice Department designed a new program based on the precept that companions influence behaviors. Children with supportive families spent time with parents and siblings, decreasing the odds of recidivism. Those children without supportive families tended to make poor choices and re-offend while in the company of the same peers who'd led them into trouble. The program purported to give these kids a second chance by severing the continued association with negative influences. The idea was to change the friends by moving the child in hopes of increasing the odds of a successful lifestyle change.

"That's right. Did you talk to the school in Pennsylvania? What's that name…Onagotchee…Onagoatee?" Ruby served as Cindy Brodan's public defender.

"Onagitchee. Onagitchee Children's Home. Yes and no. I've called, but haven't managed to reach the right teachers. You know how erratic their class schedules can be. I'll keep trying."

"Thanks. I have a few other bits of paralegal work I need you to do for me. I'll bring paperwork in a day or two, if that's okay."

"Sure. Hey, you'd better scoot if you're going to pick up the kids."

"Okay, see you later." Ruby paused in the doorway and turned back. "By the way, did Peter get over his tantrum?"

I groaned and slapped my forehead. "Oh God, I forgot to call him. He'll be twice as annoyed with me."

"Well, a little kissing up wouldn't go amiss, although honestly, Indie, I'm not sure why you bother."

"I've been doing a little wondering about that myself. Go. Get your kids."

After Ruby left, I finished picking up trash and then plunked myself into the ancient folding chair Rufus kindly lent me. The rest of the mess could wait until tomorrow. With only a couple of hours sleep, I'd done well to get this far. I pulled the clips from my hair and let it fall loose before rubbing my temples. Tomorrow I'd finish cleaning and get back to work, but first I'd visit the Oligites to offer my condolences. Maybe find out what Winston was doing in the courthouse and my office last night.

I walked home to fetch my ancient Volkswagen and then drove to the Oligite home on the outskirts of town. Nothing stirred in the entire neighborhood. A bit eerie, really. I shivered and glanced around as I pushed the doorbell. One tall oak tree in front of each run-down, but neatly kept, house. Tiny, well-tended flowerbeds. The smell of meat grilling somewhere out of sight. Not a person in view. No bicycles lying around, no skateboards. No noise. No sign of life. I remembered the last time I was here— children laughing and playing, families sitting on front porches, lawnmowers and sprinklers running. How could it change in only a few months?

I pushed the doorbell again. Someone tugged at the heavy curtains swathing the front window, undoubtedly peeking to see who rang the bell. Finally, the door opened a crack and Sylvia Oligite peered out. She was a small woman, dark hair and dark skin. Very pretty with her long eyelashes and bright blue eyes. "Ah, it's you, Ms. Stevens. Please come in." She closed the door behind me and locked it. Switching on a tiny lamp situated away from the front window, she gestured toward a worn sofa.

"Mrs. Oligite, I am so sorry about Winston. He was a good man. I know he loved you and Robert very much."

"Thank you, Ms. Stevens. Robert is having trouble accepting his father's death." She stared down at the floor and her hands twitched from her disheveled hair to the buttons on the cuff of her shirtsleeves.

"It will take time, but Robert will be okay. After all, he has a wonderful mother." Standing close to her with my arm around

22

her shoulder, I could see the new worry lines on her face. "Please call me Indie, Sylvia. We've been friends for a long time."

"Yes, thank you, Indie. May I get you something? A cup of coffee, tea?"

"I'd love a cup of coffee if you have some made. Please don't go to any trouble if you don't." I sat on the sofa and looked around the living room while I waited. A faded upholstered chair rested near a small table holding the tiny lamp providing the only light. A potted geranium stood on a small, empty bookshelf beneath the window. No pictures hung on the walls and no bowling trophies crowded the mantel over the tiny fireplace.

Sylvia pressed through the doorway bearing a chipped mug steaming with cinnamon-scented coffee. "Please excuse the old mug. It's all I have unpacked…" She set the cup on the table beside the sofa.

"Are you leaving, Sylvia?" I sipped from the mug. Delicious.

Her eyes widened and she hunched further back in the worn chair. "I, we…yes, Indie. Please do not tell anyone. I am afraid."

My cell phone vibrated in my pocket and I ignored it. "Afraid? Because of Winston's murder?"

"Yes…I mean, no. I…please, Indie, I cannot speak of this. I am sorry, but I must return to my packing. If you'll excuse me…"

"Of course, Sylvia. Thank you for the coffee and give my love to Robert." I pulled a business card from my purse and scribbled my private cell phone number on the back. "Please take this with you. Call if there's anything you or Robert need or if I can help in any way."

Lack of sleep and stress took its toll. I drove home daydreaming of a hot bath, a cup of coffee, and a bowl of soup for dinner and a bit of violin practice before bed. Instead, I got Peter.

He waited in his patrol car in front of my house. "Hey, babe, where ya been? How about we have dinner together? I get off shift in fifteen minutes. Have to drop the car at the office, but I'll come straight back."

"Peter, what are doing here? How long have you been sitting in front of my house?" A wave of weariness washed over me and I stumbled as I approached the door.

"Not long. We have orders to spend some extra patrol time in this neighborhood and I saw you coming. Figured I'd park and wait. Been thinking about your risotto all day."

"Risotto? No, I can't. I'm sorry, but I'm exhausted. I want a bath and bed. Maybe this weekend. Okay?"

He stared at me, a hurt expression on his face. "I thought you might want to spend some time together. We haven't seen much of each other all week."

Unbelievable. Last night he stormed away without a word despite what I'd been through and today he wanted me to cook for him. Forget murder and the destruction of my office. Forget someone tried to get into my house last night. Forget my lack of sleep. After all, he wanted risotto. I opened my mouth to chastise him, but snapped it shut. Maybe I was being unfair to him. "I'd love to spend time with you, but I really need a bath and some sleep."

He focused those beautiful green eyes on my face. "Are you truly that tired? Okay, you go take a bath and I'll order pizza. Okay?"

I dozed off twice in the tub, waking the second time only when I slipped beneath the water. Time to get out before I managed to drown myself. My long flannel nightgown felt heavenly, warm and cozy.

Peter had arranged plates and my favorite veggie pizza on the coffee table. I plopped into my beloved overstuffed chair and he turned on the television before covering me with the quilt I kept folded on the back of the couch. I took the proffered slice of pizza and inhaled the luscious aroma. Mushrooms, peppers, olives, and red onions. "Thanks, Pete. It smells delicious."

I think I managed half a slice before falling asleep, hardly noticing when Pete carried me to the bedroom and tucked me beneath the fluffy down comforter. The ringing of my cell phone jarred me awake at 5 a.m. "Hello?"

"Indie, wake up. Are you there?" Ruby sounded insistent, worried. "I'm going to need you this morning. Can you be in your office in an hour?"

I brushed my straggling hair from my face and shuddered at the taste of last night's pizza still in my mouth. Tiptoeing from the room to avoid waking Pete, I headed to the kitchen and poked a cup under the coffee pot. "Okay, start over. Sorry. I was sound asleep."

"Sorry. I figured you would be, but this is important. I'm going to need your help this morning with my clients."

"Why? What's going on?" I yawned and sipped from the cup. Mm, dark roast. Strong and bitter on the tongue.

"Indie, snap yourself out of it. Get some coffee or wash your face or something."

"I have coffee and I'm awake. Go on." I took another sip and let this morning's java rinse away my pizza breath.

"It's Cindy. Cindy Brodan. She's disappeared."

Chapter Three

Pete mumbled from the other side of the bed as I hopped up and down, trying to get a leg in yesterday's dirty jeans. I snagged a clean shirt from the closet as I rushed past. My hair practically stood on end, full of static because of the dry air and a night filled with tossing and turning. I gave up my futile efforts with the hairbrush and pinned it to the back of my head with two clips. Why couldn't I look elegant and polished like Ruby? Grinning at the thought of me in heels with salon-styled hair, I shoved my feet into my tennis shoes and ran all the way to my office.

The courthouse didn't open until seven, so I used my key and then, re-locked the front door after I entered. While I waited for Ruby, I made a pot of coffee and wished fervently that my files hadn't disappeared the night of the murder. Oh, my God. Why didn't I realize it earlier? I'd have to inform the Judge confidential files had disappeared from my office.

Suppressing a groan, I answered my ringing cell phone.

"Hey, come let me in." Ruby sounded cool and professional.

"On my way."

We drank coffee at my desk, sitting in the folding chairs Rufus had loaned me. "Sorry about the Styrofoam cups. Mine were smashed and I forgot to bring more."

Ruby waved a hand, the overhead light glinting from her wedding ring. "Not important. Now, what were you saying about talking to his Honor?"

"My juvie files are gone and plenty of other sealed cases. Like the sexual assault cases I've investigated. Most of those were Oldham's cases. I need to tell him what happened."

"Yes, you're right. Well, surely his Honor can't be angry with you." Ruby dismissed the idea of trouble with another elegant wave of her hand. "Okay, on to poor Cindy's story. Here are the replacement files I brought for you. I'll check later to see if I have others, but for now concentrate on Cindy. You're acting as my paralegal in this and I want you to find out everything you can."

"Sure, but what happened? Where is she?"

"According to the sheriff's department, she managed to run away from the group home in Pennsylvania and cadge her way onto a bus. She disappeared somewhere between there and here."

"You want me to look for her?"

"Of course not. That's the sheriff's job. No, I want you to re-read the file and be available to collect information from the deputies. I'll be in Shrewsdale all week at the G.A.L. conference and I need someone trustworthy acting in my stead. I gave your name to the sheriff as my paralegal. If you don't hear from them in a day or so, call them."

"Will do. You know, my mom lives in Pennsylvania. She's been after me for a long time to visit her. If I flew down to see her,

I could visit the school where the court sent Cindy. Maybe I'll find out more than I could in a telephone conversation."

"That would be great. We'll figure it out later, okay? I need to review some documents before I meet with my client." She tossed her Styrofoam cup in the trash. "Thanks for the coffee."

I sat at my desk, thinking about Cindy Brodan, a beautiful, but troubled and self-destructive teenager. Her parents willingly surrendered her to the legal system, wearied of the constant drama. A stint in a group home under constant supervision seemed a perfect solution, although I had reservations about sending children out of state.

Voices sounded in the hallway outside my office and I looked at my watch. Seven a.m., time for the courthouse to open. In an effort to save money, the county closed its offices every Friday. Employees now worked four ten-hour days, which made long working days, but also long weekends. The early and late hours proved beneficial to those county residents who got off work at 5 p.m. and needed to pay property taxes or buy automobile license plates.

However, the parking lot wasn't usually crowded so early in the morning. I scrunched down in my folding chair, trying to watch the activity without conspicuously spying. A dozen deputies stood in a group involved in what appeared a serious conversation. While I looked (okay, spied on the participants), several cars from the neighboring county sheriff's department pulled into the parking lot and screeched to a halt, disgorging additional law enforcement personnel. Judge Beecher Oldham stood near Wayne Muley, our local Sheriff, who leaned close as if His Honor spoke in low tones.

Wow, must be some big shindig to convince Muley to ask for help from another county and especially big to drag Oldham out of his manor at this early hour. Even the ungodly time of day hadn't deterred him from taking time to dress well. His starched white shirt gleamed in the rising sun and light glinted from his cufflinks. As I watched, he brushed at the sleeve of his suit jacket and straightened his tie.

Could this have something to do with Cindy's disappearance? I glanced at my watch, wishing I had a plausible reason for ambling into the midst of the conclave. Ah-ha! Just what I needed...Peter getting out of his patrol car. Tucking my shirttail into my jeans, I scrambled down the hall and out the door to the parking lot.

I poked my arm under his and scooted close. "Hey, you. Thanks for the pizza and for tucking me into bed. I feel much better this morning."

He gave me one of his most heart-melting smiles and kissed the top of my head. "Hey, even I, insensitive male that I am, could tell you were worn out."

I laughed. "Well, thanks again. What's all the commotion?"

"Ha! I wondered why you came out. Had a feeling it wasn't just to see me." He fluttered his eyelashes, making me laugh again.

"Hey, Pete, the Sheriff wants us in his office." Shawn Trellicki, Peter's friend since high school and fellow deputy, waved before climbing into his patrol car and driving out of the parking lot.

"Gotta run, Babe. See you tonight?" He shook his head. "I don't know how the guy keeps going. He worked the night shift and has been out here for hours already, searching for that girl."

"Cindy? Is that what this law enforcement confab is about?"

"Yes, the girl who disappeared from the bus." He snapped his fingers. "You and Ruby had the juvie case, didn't you? Thought so. The Sheriff wanted to meet with all deputies to discuss search plans. He and Shawn heard about it first and started looking for her, but all these guys have volunteered to help whenever they're off duty."

My heart ached at the thought of the troubled girl alone somewhere, frightened, possibly hurt or even abducted. "You'll let me know if you hear anything?"

"Of course I will." He leaned down and gave me a deeply satisfying kiss, but broke off with a grin at the sound of loud catcalls from his coworkers. "Tonight?"

No mistaking the intent behind the question. I returned his leer. "Definitely."

"Hampton, get going before the Sheriff decides to skin you alive." Captain Rolly Peterson gestured toward Pete's car.

"I'm going, I'm going." He turned those gorgeous eyes in my direction again. "Tonight."

I headed back to my office on weak knees. It happened every time he turned on the charm factor. How could a woman resist?

Settling in my folding chair with a cup of fresh coffee, I inhaled deeply, letting the fragrant vapor flood my senses. The thick file before me presented a daunting sight. Two volumes, both massive. The poor kid had been in the courtroom more times than I cared to count.

"Volume One" required two hours to read. I stretched in the folding chair and wriggled my rear end, trying to get some feeling back. Time to get up and move a bit before continuing. I started the coffee brewer and walked to the window while it did its thing. Nothing much happening in the parking lot. A few customers going in and out, probably to renew their license plates. Somebody's black lab barking from the back of a pickup truck. Deputy Shawn Trellicki talking to the Sheriff. Rufus and his assistant mowing the lawn.

I shrugged. No more lollygagging. Onward to "Volume Two."

Three and a half hours later, I pushed my folding chair away from the desk and shook my head. Sometimes a person just couldn't fathom a situation. The Brodan family seemed normal in all respects, except for the troubled child. Father, Barty, owner of a small auto parts store. Mother, Marion, part-time librarian. Both parents seemed kind, loving and concerned for their daughter's welfare. Cindy's three-year old brother Joshua had started nursery school this year and Marion volunteered part-time as a class helper.

How could a loving home produce a child who ended up in the juvenile system? Every time I'd seen her, Cindy looked desperate and wild. No, that wasn't quite right. More like desperate and terrified. Yes, that was the right word, terrified. Maybe she feared confinement in a group home. Rumors did circulate among teenagers.

Time to quit for the day. I'd re-read the reports from the Pennsylvania school tomorrow. No hurry now, since there would be no hearing unless somebody found Cindy. I pulled the clips from my hair and rubbed my temples. Stupid things gave me a headache. Maybe I should shave my head. Ha! Wouldn't that startle everyone?

Okay, time to check with the sheriff's department for news on the missing girl-no news, except searchers continued to comb the area along the bus route without luck- and then, head home for something to eat before band practice tonight-a bowl of cereal.

The old Volkswagen fired right up and I patted the dashboard, ignoring an odd ticking noise from under the hood, before backing out of my tiny garage to head to Steve's place.

Steve Morrison, who played guitar, had a huge shop remodeled into a rather nice sound room. It made a great practice room. We frequently recorded ourselves and used the tapes as a guide to improvement.

I parked on the wide shoulder of his driveway and groaned as I realized I was the last to arrive. Again. Large, dark clouds obscured the normally bright evening sun as I grabbed my violin case from the trunk.

The rhythmic thud of Gerry's stand-up bass sounded through the door and a faint odor of charred meat and smoke filled the air. I couldn't help grinning. Anita, Steve's wife, insisted on doing the family barbequing, but didn't quite have the hang of it yet.

A noticeable tension filled the huge room and I looked around, trying to figure out the problem. Steve sat in an old wooden chair, an electronic tuner on his knees, tuning his Martin D10. Brady, our talented and slightly pudgy banjo player, drank a diet soda. Both men rolled their eyes to their left.

Ah, I saw it now. Gerry stood unsteadily next to his stand-up bass, holding a beer in his left hand while plunking an occasional string with the right. The neck of the instrument wobbled from one shoulder to the other and balanced precariously against his chest. Half a dozen empty beer cans littered the floor and a nearby table held several full six-packs plus an empty carton.

Past time we did something about the drinking problem. It proved an embarrassment on more than one occasion, shortening our playing time at gigs when his musical ability declined as the number of beers consumed rose. Last summer we barely kept up with the flood of requests rolling in for the band to play. This year, word of Gerry's "problem" spread and the flood dwindled to a trickle. What could we do? Stand-up bass players are hard to find and what's a bluegrass band without its bass?

"Let's roll, guys. I need to get an early start tomorrow." I sat my case on a table and pulled out the violin and bow. "Everyone ready?"

Gerry slurped the last of his beer and tossed the can on the floor, wiping his mouth with the back of his hand. "Howsh…how about a little Foggy Mountain Breakdown to get the blood flowing?"

"He couldn't make it through the first measure, let alone the entire tune."

I was the only one close enough to hear Steve's whispered words. Hoping to avoid the usual argument, I ignored the comment. "Let's try a waltz first, okay? Gives me time to limber up."

We moved from my favorite waltz to faster numbers. After I did a bit of showing off with my newest rendition of "Orange Blossom Special," Steve did some of his fine picking on "Black Mountain Rag." By then we'd been at it for over two hours, so the appearance of Anita bearing a tray of snacks provided a welcome diversion.

She planted a kiss on Steve's cheek. "You want to run in and grab the coffee carafe and cups for me? Thanks. Hi, Indie. I heard about what happened at the courthouse. It must have been a terrible experience for you."

"Pretty awful. Poor Winston Oligite. He was such a nice man." Gratefully, I accepted the proffered cup of coffee and one of Anita's wonderful, still-warm chocolate chip cookies. "Mmm. Delicious. Thanks."

"You're welcome. At least they're more edible than my barbecued creations. Well, I'll leave all of you to get back to playing." She paused at the door and turned sideways, giving me a signal with a pointing finger.

Now that she gave me the idea, I realized I had the creepy feeling of someone standing too near. Gerry had propped his bass against a convenient bench and moved just behind me.

"You want something? A cookie, maybe?" I didn't like him very much, but he was a fine bass player when he wasn't drunk.

Even though he now drank from a cup of strong coffee, Gerry reeked of alcohol. "No, I don't want a damned cookie. Too bad you had to go and get mixed up in it."

I took a step backward, hoping to get out of range of the fumes. "Mixed up in what? Are you referring to the murder in my office? I am hardly mixed up in it."

"See it stays that way. My wife wouldn't have been hanging around a murderer, not if she was still here." He slammed the coffee cup on the tray and yanked another beer from the case. The loud pop of the pull-tab alerted Steve and Brady.

"Hey, slow down, buddy. Let's get back to work." Steve strummed a G-chord on his guitar.

We managed another hour of practice before Gerry's playing became too erratic to continue. After the events of the last few days, I really needed a good night's sleep anyway. "I think I've had enough for one night. How about you guys?"

"Yeah, I'm bushed. Long day in the salt mines." Brady worked as a systems analyst for a computer company. "C'mon, Gerry. I'll give you a ride home."

Steve and Brady took turns driving when Gerry drank too much, which was almost every day. I tried taking a turn once last year, but refused to do it again because Gerry slobbered all over me the whole way to his house.

My car started right up, but the ticking noise was louder.

"You want me to take a look at that? You could pull it into the garage." Steve frowned as he leaned over the hood, listening to the engine.

"No, but thanks. I'll take it into the shop tomorrow. See ya, Steve. Tell Anita thanks again for the cookies."

"Will do." He waved and headed into the house.

About two miles down the road, the ticking increased in volume. In another moment the noise stopped. Because the engine died.

I looked at the large raindrops spattering the windshield and slumped against the seat back. This made the third time in a year that I'd run out of gas. Why couldn't I remember to check the gauge before driving?

Thank God for cell phones. I grabbed mine from the passenger seat and used the touch screen to call Peter's number. It took a moment for me to realize I heard no ring. No service bars. The growing storm had probably knocked out something or other. Hmm, two miles back to Steve's and the same distance to town. No sense sitting in the car freezing and so few cars traveled this road at night I had almost zero chance of finding a ride. Despite the coming storm, I'd have to walk home.

I climbed out of the car and locked my violin in the trunk. Didn't want to carry it in the rain and risk water damage, but also figured tempting thieves wasn't a good idea. Hard to replace a good violin. Expensive, too.

I had just tucked the keys in my pocket when I noticed headlights coming from the hill behind me. Had to be one of the guys. No, wait…they'd all left before me. Maybe Steve or Anita? No, they'd gone to bed. I'd seen the lights turn off in their house as I pulled out of the driveway.

No matter. Anyone out driving on a night like this would be a friend of mine if they'd pulled over and gave me a lift. I wrapped my arms around my chest, trying to still the shivering. The rain fell harder and lightening flashed in the distance. In the absolute blackness of the night, the headlights travelled slowly, weaving from one side of the road to the other. Probably somebody heading home from a bar in the next town. Riding with an inebriated driver wasn't my first choice of transport, but maybe the driver was dodging potholes.

Watching the car's tortuous progress, I figured I had at least another ten minutes before it reached me. Waiting inside my car would take me out of the wind, which now blew with real violence. I struggled to reach the driver's door over clay soil now slick from the sudden downpour. After a few steps, thick mud coated the bottoms of my shoes. The wind whipped my hair loose, flinging the clips into the darkness along with my glasses. Half-blinded by the lack of glasses and the sodden mass now hanging in my face, I could only feel, not see, the door handle beneath my shaking hand.

Locked. Dammit. Could things get any worse? Alone in the pitch black, I could hear tree branches snap as they broke in the vicious wind. What an idiot I'd been. Why hadn't I checked the gas gauge? Brady had offered earlier to give me a lift.

I smelled ozone as I jammed a hand in my pocket, searching for the keys. Just as my fingertips touched the familiar shape, I slipped and landed face down in the slimy mud. Oh, God. Now things were truly miserable. My whole body shuddered with cold. Where was the car I'd seen? Mud obscured my vision and I wiped the worst of it from my eyes.

Finally tearing the other hand free from my pocket, I managed to yank out the keys and drag myself to my knees by grasping the door handle. The wind howled like a wolf at moonrise and rain fell in great sheets. I tilted my head upward for a moment, letting the mud slough from my face. Jamming the keys into the door-lock, I let go of the car and used both hands to tug at one mud-trapped foot. It popped free with a loud sucking noise and I held it above the mud, poised to lift it into the car.

A monumental flash of lightening burst right above me, illuminating a landscape made bizarre by the storm. Trees bent and cracked, leaves whipping in the wind. The clay soil of the road had become a river of mud, slowly flowing downhill.

The boom of thunder startled me and I fell again, this time backward into the sea of muck. Something whizzed over me and struck the driver's door with an explosive pinging sound. Even without my eyeglasses, I recognized it before the brilliant flash of lightening died away.

A bullet hole now adorned the old Volkswagen.

Chapter Four

Whiz. Ping.

This time, the bullet struck only slightly above my head. I heard the hiss of escaping air and knew it must've nicked a tire. Would a tire explode if a bullet hit it fully? I'd ask Peter the next time I...what's was wrong with me? My brain must be suffering from the loss of body heat. Focus. I needed to focus on my current problems and forget about questions.

First order of business...get out of here. The slippery clay afforded no purchase for my clutching fingers, so I dug in with my elbows, pulling myself around the back to the passenger side of the car. I lay still for a moment, trying to catch my breath, but all the while, my heart thudded in my chest. Terrified the next lightening flash would reveal someone standing over me with a gun, I decided to make a run for the trees.

Amend that—a *crawl* for the trees. The mud caked on the bottoms of my shoes made it impossible to stand, although it probably saved my life because the shooter hadn't given up. I heard several shots zing in the general direction of my car. Thankfully, visibility was near zero.

Swallowing bile and scarcely able to breathe, I dragged myself by my now-battered elbows to the nearest growth of trees ten feet off the road. With that small measure of protection between my would-be killer and me, I sat and leaned against a tree to remove my shoes. Most of the mud yielded to scraping against tree bark and I stuffed them back on my feet, sans the caked and useless laces.

Terror had driven away all cognizance of cold, but it now returned with vengeance. Oh my God, I'd never been so cold in my life. My teeth chattered and my body shook so violently I had to move away from my supporting tree for fear of breaking my own back. If I stayed here, I would die of hypothermia. I had to move.

Keeping the vague image of the road in sight, I struggled to half walk, half crawl, parallel to the road. I clung for a few moments to the trunk of every tree I passed, pressing my face to the bark and inhaling the pine scent. The aroma had a calming effect and the brief respite every few minutes gave me strength.

The storm weakened. A misty rain continued to fall, but the wind died down. The eerie darkness enveloped me, hid me. Gave me a crazy sense of well-being. No more bullets flew past.

Hoping the shooter had given up, I moved toward the road, but stopped when I spotted something under a bush. *If it's a blanket, I'm wrapping myself in it. I don't care if it's filthy, soaking wet and covered with spiders.* I tugged, but couldn't pull it free. Refusing to give up, I stuck my head into the bush, feeling around to find what snagged it.

It wasn't a blanket and it wasn't snagged. It was clothing. Clothing on a body. A dead body.

Cindy Brodan.

Chapter Five

The bus traveled this road daily, so I *knew* searchers had combed this area. *How could they have missed her?* Finding Cindy's body added a layer of horror to the misery and terror I felt. A giant lump formed in my throat and I knew it would soon erupt in a loud wail.

No, I couldn't fall to pieces now. I had to hang on, to find someone to retrieve the poor girl's body and to help me. The road lay only a short distance to my left and I'd heard something earlier. My beleaguered brain struggled to remember.

Voices. I'd heard voices. Salvation lay with finding someone to help.

I stumbled, fell and crawled to the edge of the forest, feeling as if I traveled an eternity. Twice, I'd dropped to my knees to find my lace-less shoe when it slipped off my foot. I no longer shivered and I knew that was a bad sign. My body had given up its efforts to warm me.

The wind carried the sound of a conversation to my ears. I only caught intermittent words, "went wild" and "might find." Gasping with the effort of moving under the weight of mud and water encasing my jeans, I stopped to catch my breath and listen. If I didn't recognize the voices, how would I know whether it was the shooter?

Thank God, I knew that voice—Shawn. Peter's partner, Shawn Trellicki, spoke to someone. "You fool!" The wind whipped away the rest of his words, but I didn't care.

My first attempt to call his name came out as a weak croak. I stumbled another foot closer and tried again. "Shawn, help me."

The clouds scudded apart and a moonbeam flashed on the figure of Shawn, his fist poised as if to strike someone. I didn't see who it was and I didn't care. "Help me."

Darkness closed over us again, but Shawn had seen me. "Indie? Is that you?" He grabbed my arm.

Twin headlights traveling toward us illuminated everything; my Volkswagen, the sea of mud, the patrol vehicle parked on the other side of the road. Shawn dropped my arm as the car stopped and Peter climbed out.

"Hey, what's going on, partner?" Peter climbed out, leaving the engine running. "Oh, my God! Indie, what happened?"

The headlights on Peter's car lit Shawn's scowl. I knew him only casually, but knew he and Peter worked well together. Right now, I felt like hugging him in gratitude. "Thank you, thank you for finding me."

"Lucky for you I was assigned to patrol this area. We normally don't, you know, but we're still looking for that teenager." Shawn's voice held a note of strain, which I attributed to worry over the missing girl, Cindy.

Cindy, oh my God, I'd forgotten about her. I burst into tears.

"Hey, everything will be fine now. Let's get you home." Recoiling slightly at the feel of mud and muck, Peter put an arm around me and steered me toward his car.

"No, wait." The cold hit me again and I began shaking so hard that I struggled to speak. "Wait."

"You can tell me later. C'mon, Indie. Get in the car. Thanks again, Shawn. I'll call you later, after I get her home." A blast of heat rolled out of the car door Peter yanked open.

"Cindy." My chattering teeth drowned out my voice.

"What did you say?" Peter pushed me into the back seat and pulled a silver blanket from the emergency kit kept under the driver's seat. He shut my door and climbed into the car. "Here, put this on, too."

Struggling into the fleece jacket he handed to me, I watched Shawn's taillights disappear in the direction of town and tried again. "Cindy. In the woods. Over there."

"What?" Peter whipped around in his seat, eyes wide. "You saw Cindy? Where is she? You left her in the woods? Is she injured?"

Shaking my head, I tried to concentrate. The warmth enveloped me, soothed me, and nearly lulled me to sleep. My voice came out in a whisper. "No. No, she's dead in those trees over there."

"Where? Can you show me where? No, no. Don't try to get up. Just point." He called Shawn on the radio, asking him to return and then radioed dispatch, notifying them of my report.

A car approached, but it came from the wrong direction for it to be Shawn. "Hey, what's going on? Pete, is that you in there?" I recognized Steve's voice, but not the vehicle.

Peter hung up the radio and rolled down his window. "Hello, Steve. Yeah, it's me, Peter. I've got Indie in here, too."

"Indie? She left a long time ago. I..." He swiveled his head and his voice rose. "Oh my God, that's her car, isn't it? What happened? Did she have an accident? Is she okay?"

"I'm fine, Steve. No accident. Just ran out of gas." I sat up so he could see for himself that I was in one piece.

"You should've let me look at that engine. Anita will never forgive me."

"No need. The engine wasn't the problem. I ran out of gas, so I tried to walk home and the storm caught me. What are you doing out here? I thought you went to bed."

Steve growled. "I did. It's Gerry again."

"Gerry? But, Brady drove him home."

"Correction—Brady *tried* to drive him home, but Gerry jumped out when the car slowed. Yelled something about getting his car and being tired of everyone treating him like a baby. Brady called from town and asked if I'd help look for him. That was some time ago because I had to go back and get Anita's station wagon. I had a flat on my Jeep and didn't notice until I reached the top of the hill."

"Ah, that was you I saw earlier, before..." Something clicked, but no way. I refused to consider Steve as the shooter.

"Before what?"

"Nothing. I'm just tired and don't know what I'm saying." I leaned against the seat back.

"Okay, well, I'm heading home to try calling Brady. Maybe I'll be lucky and that damned Gerry will have showed up somewhere so I can go to bed, too." He waved at Peter before climbing back into his car and heading toward his house.

I huddled in the back seat under the emergency blanket, miserable and shivering despite the heat blasting at me from the front of the car. When headlights approached and Peter opened his door to join Shawn, I panicked. "No! Don't go anywhere. Please don't leave me alone."

"What? It's fine, Indie. I'll be back in a few minutes."

"You don't understand, Peter. Someone…" My voice had returned, but my dry mouth refused to work properly. "Someone tried to kill me. Go look. There's a bullet hole on the driver's side."

He flicked on the dim overhead light and stared at me. Without a word, he opened the door and crossed the muddy road to my car. His flashlight beam traveled up and down the Volkswagen. He leaned over to pluck something from the mud and then, stopped to confer with Shawn before returning to the car. "Here you go. I found your glasses, but you'll have to wash them before you can wear them. I've called in backup to help with Cindy. We're going home."

"Wait. My violin. Please get my violin from the trunk."

Even in the shadows produced by the dome light, I could see his jaw clench. Without speaking, he strode back to my car, retrieved the keys from the driver's door and removed the case from the trunk.

With the violin in my hands, a wave of relief washed over me. For the first time since I'd stepped out of my car, my heart beat normally and I breathed easily. I pulled the silver blanket tighter, curled up on the seat, and fell asleep.

****

I awoke late the next day, clean and rested, with a vague memory of Peter carrying me into my house. My hair smelled fresh and I wore warm flannel pajamas, so he undoubtedly bathed me and put me to bed. *How could a person sleep through that?* The thought of coffee lured me to the kitchen, where I found a note beside the brewer.

Indie,

Call me when you wake & I'll pick you up. We towed your car to the County shop for examination & the sheriff wants to ask you some questions.

Love,

Peter

After three cups of dark-roast and a shower, I felt able to face another round of questioning. I called Peter and waited inside until I heard him honk his horn.

After I climbed into his car, he peered intently into my eyes. "Good morning. You look much better. How do you feel?"

"Sore muscles, a few scratches. I'm fine." A sudden vision hit me—poor Cindy Brodan, lying under the brush beside the road into town. I swallowed before continuing. "What happened to Cindy? Has there been an autopsy?"

Peter put an arm around my shoulder. "The coroner is working on it."

"You've heard nothing?"

He hesitated. "You may as well hear it from me. I'm sorry, Indie, but unofficially, she was murdered. There are ligature marks around her neck consistent with strangulation."

The terrors of the night returned and nearly overwhelmed me. Bullets flying overhead, lightening flashing, thunder booming. Worst of all, a beautiful, young girl lying motionless in the brush beside a road. I shivered as if stranded in the storm again. *Who could do this? Why would anyone do such a terrible, terrible thing?*

"I'm sorry, Indie. I know how much you and Ruby wanted to help the girl."

I brushed tears from my cheeks and looked into his handsome face. "Thanks, Peter. Does the sheriff have any leads, any ideas?"

He seemed troubled as he gave me a hug. "No, nothing yet, but we had to wait till morning to start knocking on doors and questioning people."

"What is it? Something's wrong. I can tell."

"I went to the shop this morning to look at your car."

"Yes?" I watched Peter's face as he hesitated.

"I found the bullet hole, alright. Three of them, actually."

"C'mon, what's with you? Why do I feel like I have to pry information out of you?"

He shook his head as if shaking loose a bad memory. "Okay, now don't get all excited, but you didn't run out of gas."

"Of course I did. I certainly didn't decide to stroll home during a storm."

"No, that's not what I mean. Your car definitely quit running, but gasoline wasn't the problem. Someone pulled the plug, drained the oil and then replaced the plug. Your car stopped because there was no oil in the engine. It's ruined, burned up." He pulled into the courthouse parking lot and parked the car.

I returned his stare. "The ticking noise. Are you saying it was deliberate? I don't believe it. I probably forgot to check the oil or something. The same way I forget to check the gas gauge. Why would anyone do something like that?"

"No, maybe you forgot to check the gas gauge, but I changed your oil two days ago. I *know* your car had oil. There are no leaks, so there's no other explanation. Someone deliberately drained the oil."

"But, why? That makes no sense."

"I don't know, but I intend to find out. I'm hoping to get prints off the oil plug. C'mon, I'll walk you to the office and then, I've got to get back to work."

Shawn Trellicki and Sheriff Wayne Muley held an animated conversation in the sheriff's office. Peter rapped on the glass door before opening it. "Here she is, sir. You ready to hit the road, Shawn?"

"See you, boys. Stay safe out there." The sheriff waited until Shawn and Peter left and then closed the glass door. "Have a seat, Indie."

I plopped myself into the plastic chair he indicated and looked at him. Sheriff Wayne Muley inspired confidence in most people. Well over six feet tall, he was a big man with an air of benign authority. His daily uniform consisted of khaki pants, shirt and a wide-brim cowboy hat. With his salt-and-pepper mustache, he exuded maturity and level-headedness, a fitting demeanor for his position.

"Now, I understand you had a spot of trouble last night and that's how you discovered Cindy Brodan's body." Wayne pulled the unlit cigar from his mouth and carefully placed it in the spotless ashtray on his desk. Several months ago, he began chewing the things, instead of smoking them, at the insistence of his wife, Molly. "You ran out of gas on your way home from Steve Morrison's place. That right?"

I shook my head. "That's what I thought, but Peter said no. He said someone tampered with the oil plug."

"We-e-ll, Peter's a man in love, looking for bogies under every bush, you know. Let's leave that issue aside for now. Tell me about these so-called shots. Peter said you think someone shot at you."

"Yes, I had thought of trying to walk home when my car quit running, but the wind and rain were terrible. I decided to get back into the car, but just as I got the key into the door lock, I slipped. Something whizzed past my head as I fell. There was a second shot as I lay in the mud."

"Now, in all that noise, isn't it possible you imagined the sound of a bullet? Little thing like you gets mighty spooked in a big ol' storm like that. Besides, nobody could hear clearly in that much of a racket. I was right here in this office and I could hardly hear myself think."

My face grew hot. "No, I didn't imagine it. There are three bullet holes to prove it."

He smoothed his mustache with a fingertip and picked up the cigar. "Now, little lady, don't get yourself worked up. We're still looking at the car, so there's no proof those little marks are bullet holes. I can't just take your word for it. Maybe you banged that car into your garage wall or something and didn't notice until now."

"Little marks? I *heard* a bullet fly past my head and I *heard* it hit my car."

"Now, don't get all hysterical all me, Indie. Let's talk about something else. Did you see anyone? Hear anyone moving around?"

I leaped from the chair and put both hands on the edge of Muley's desk. "I'm not hysterical, but I *am* angry. I came to this office of my own free will because Peter said you had questions. I did not come here to be treated like a child having a nightmare. This is crazy. I'm leaving."

I stomped toward the door, but the sheriff beat me to it. Chomping furiously on his cigar, he stretched out a hand to hold the door shut. "Hold on there. I don't know why you're so upset. Just sit back and let's start again. I want you to tell me about finding Cindy Brodan's body."

The thought of poor Cindy deflated my anger. Perching on the edge of the chair, I crossed my arms over my chest and waited without speaking.

"Now, did you see anything suspicious in the area where you found the body?" Muley once again rested his cigar in the ashtray. "You sure you didn't see anyone hanging around?"

"Hanging around? In the middle of the night and during the worst storm we've had in almost fifty years? First you tell me the storm frightened me so badly that I imagined someone trying to shoot me, but now, despite the same storm, you think I can give evidence?" *What the hell is going on here? Someone shot at me, Cindy is dead and the sheriff is only interested in asking stupid questions.*

"Okay, Indie, maybe you should go home and get some rest. I know you must be tired after your experience last night." He rose from his chair and gestured toward the door. "I've got a meeting to attend right now, but we'll call you when we've finished with your car. If you think of anything, you give us a call."

I walked home, too dispirited to even check on my office.

Chapter Six

"Mom, is that you?" I thought talking with my mother might provide some prospective or at least a morale boost, but the background noise at her number nearly drowned out her voice.

"Yes, it's me, Indie dear. Sorry about the noise. Hang up and I'll call you right back, okay?"

My phone rang a moment later. "Hi, Mom. How are you and what's the racket?"

She laughed and I knew exactly how she must look, brushing her greying hair back from her temples as her face creased with its perpetual smile. "I'm fine, dear and so is Daddy. He's off on his annual fishing trip with Bob Lorden. I'm afraid I'm up to my annual remodeling."

I grinned at the thought of my father's pretended chagrin every year when he returned from fishing to find at least one room in their home entirely unrecognizable. Each year he asked my mother why she didn't just buy or build a new house, if she thought so many things required change. She always replied that she loved *this* house and it just needed a bit of a touch-up. Her touch-ups generally required knocking out walls and tearing up floors, most accomplished by herself despite her tiny size. I laughed. "Send pictures when you've finished."

She agreed with a giggle and then sobered. "How are you, dear? I heard about that poor Mr. Oligite. Lucille keeps me informed, you know."

Lucille Marcus lived only half a mile from me. She and my mother remained best friends despite half a country between them. "Have you talked to her today?"

"No, she's visiting her sister in Omaha this week. Is something wrong, dear? Has something else happened?"

I told her about leaving band practice and my car running out of gas during the big storm. "When I stumbled through the woods, I found a missing girl, a girl I knew."

"Knew?" Pretty sharp, my mother.

"Yes, a sixteen year old girl who disappeared. I found her body in some bushes."

She gasped and then asked, "Indie, why were you wandering about the woods?"

I hesitated. If I didn't tell her now, she'd probably hear it from Lucille. Bullet holes are hard to hide, even when the sheriff refuses to admit their existence, and juicy gossip travels like wildfire in a small town. On the other hand, mothers worry. It's part of their job description, but I hated to add to it. "Okay, Mom, remember that I'm fine. Promise you won't panic?"

"Indianetta Stevens, you tell me what's going on. Right now."

The note of firmness jolted me back to childhood. After all, I'd called seeking comfort. My story poured forth without pause, like a wild river escaping the confines of its banks. When I stopped to breathe, I realized my mother hadn't said a word.

"Mom, are you still there?"

"Indie, I want you to come home. You need to get away to a safe place. Leave the investigation to the police. Come home."

I considered the idea. It proved tempting—a nice long vacation without responsibility or worry. Other than helping with her remodeling projects, my mother always insisted I use my time with her to relax, visit friends, make a few fun shopping trips. "It sounds like a great idea, Mom. It's been too long since I've seen you and Dad, but it will be a week or two before I can leave. I'll let you know."

"Come as soon as you can, Indie. This situation frightens me. I don't understand any of it." She sounded on the verge of tears.

"I'll be there soon. I promise." A wave of homesickness washed over me. I missed them both—my energetic mother and my indulgent father. Not for the first time, I wished they hadn't moved so far away when they retired. After swearing to call her once a day, I hung up the phone and made a cup of strong coffee.

I sat at my kitchen table to do some thinking. With so few crimes normally occurring in our small town, two murders in such a short time seemed unbelievable. Two crimes…did that mean two criminals, two murderers, running loose or did one person commit both? That looked more likely to me or maybe it was just easier to swallow the idea of one crazy person.

Wincing at the thought of Peter's remonstrance, I sipped from my cup and lit a cigarette. He never failed to lecture me on the ills of cigarettes when he detected the odor of smoke. Not that he's wrong, but who wants a lecture from a boyfriend?

Time to stop wasting the remainder of the day. I typed my "to do" list into my cell phone.

1. Check on my car. Can I have it back and is it driveable?
2. Inquire about autopsy results.
3. Visit Clerk of Court office to finish research for Tom Brown.
4. Go to band practice.

The last item on the list made me shiver. Our last practice hadn't ended well for me, but we had an important gig coming up soon and we couldn't afford to slack off. Several good local bands meant fierce competition for the best jobs. Since we managed to land the big fair job this year, we'd practiced almost obsessively, hoping for a repeat next year. We all played because we loved the music, but for some of us, the money supplemented an uncertain income.

I rinsed out my coffee cup and walked back to the sheriff's office. Lila May, the sweet and elderly receptionist, smiled and spoke in her frail voice. "Hi, Indie. Looking for Pete?"

"No, actually I came to find out about my car. Have they finished checking it? I'd like to get it back."

She brushed back a wisp of white hair and frowned. "Get it back? I don't understand."

"My car. Muley kept it to investigate the bullet holes, but it's the only car I have and I need it back."

"Oh my, I don't know anything about bullet holes, but the wrecker hauled your car off to the crusher an hour ago. Didn't they tell you?"

"Hauled it away? I don't understand. Sheriff Muley was supposed to notify me when they finished the investigation so I could pick it up."

"Oh dear, I hope I'm not to blame. Maybe the sheriff expected me to call you. I certainly don't remember him asking me to phone anyone." Her brow creased and she gave a nervous pat to the bun on top of her head.

"Where's Muley? I want to talk to him."

"Now don't get upset, dear. I'm sure it's a misunderstanding."

"I'm not upset with you, Lila May, but I want to talk to Muley. Now."

Peter swept into the office, a wide grin on his face. "Hey, Gorgeous. No, not you, Indie. I was talking to Lila May."

Believe it or not, the sweet old lady blushed, bringing a breath of color to her wrinkled cheeks. "I declare, Peter, you are a bold young man. Now you take your fiancé outside and explain about her car. I do wish people would tell me these things."

Peter blew a kiss in Lila May's direction and tucked my arm under his. As soon as we were outside, I glanced at him. "Fiancé?"

"Well, you know. Lila May saw my car at your house and she doesn't like the idea of people 'living in sin.' I just thought I'd ease her mind. You don't mind, do you?" He tugged my arm to pull me closer.

Maybe I'm crazy, but I *did* mind. "Peter, we've talked about this a dozen times. You know I have no marriage plans and I thought you didn't either."

His jaw muscles twitched. "Indie, I've told you that I want a family."

An older couple passed us on the sidewalk. Bearing a vehicle tag notification, they walked through the front door of the courthouse, glancing back once at us.

Feeling a rush of heat to my face, I shook my head. "Let's not argue now, not in public. Besides, I want to know what happened to my car."

"Your car?"

"Yes, my car. Lila May said the wrecker hauled it off to be crushed. What the hell is going on? Muley was supposed to call me when they finished with it."

A scowl distorted his face. "I don't know, but I'll find out. I'll call you later, okay?"

"Sure, yeah. I have some work to do in the office and some errands to run, but you can call my cell phone. Let me know what you find out." I watched him disappear through the door into the sheriff's office. Even in the beginning, we'd argued over everything. Where to eat, when to sleep, who should drive. The more time we spent together, the more our disagreements escalated. Democrat or Republican, church or no church, marriage or not. Why did two people who cared about one another have so many differences? I shrugged and headed to the Clerk of Court office.

No prisoners sat in the chair outside the courtroom and no soon-to-be divorced couples glared at one another from opposite sides of the hall. No lights shone in Judge Oldham's office. I nodded in satisfaction. Much easier to conduct research on days without court hearings.

I glanced inside the venerable, old courtroom. Sunlight gleamed on the polished wood chairs and the imposing judge's bench. It gave me the shivers to think of all the people who had waited here in trepidation for decisions affecting their lives. Thank God, I'd never been in a courtroom except as an observer.

I headed for the public access terminal and typed in the name of Tom Brown's client. Although he hadn't said much, Tom was representing his client in a custody case and I had a hunch he worried the guy might have an undisclosed felony or two. My guess and Tom's worry proved well founded. I discovered one conviction for burglary and another for assault.

The elderly Clerk of Court, Clara Hofstedder, sat at her desk signing documents. She kept her white hair pinned up and her hems way down. I'd never seen her wear anything but dark dresses and clunky shoes with square heels, like those my great-grandmother wore. In her mid-seventies, she projected an image of antique propriety. I wouldn't have been surprised to see an antimacassar on the back of her chair and a doily on her desk, but make no mistake-the woman's mind is sharp.

"Good day, Miss Stevens. May I help you?"

"Yes, please, Mrs. Hofstedder. I need copies of the felony information and the Judgment & Sentence for these two cases." I handed over the scrap of paper with the scribbled case numbers.

Four of her five deputy clerks kept their eyes glued to their work. The fifth, Gloria Smith, a younger version of Rhoda Bellinger who happened to be Gerry Marner's cousin, glared at me. "Would you like me to make those copies, Mrs. Hofstedder?"

"Why, thank you, Gloria. Yes, I need to finish these reports and that would be very helpful." Clara handed over the case numbers and returned to her desk.

"You know there's a charge for these copies." The malice in Gloria's voice stayed just far enough below the surface to avoid alarming Clara.

"Yes, I'm aware of the charge." I smiled sweetly. The woman had disliked me from the moment we met at a county retirement party several years ago. I'd given up trying to befriend her when I learned of her relationship to Rhoda Bellinger. Second cousins or something like that, which also made her Gerry's cousin.

After paying for the copies and saying goodbye to Clara, I walked across town to leave the documents with Tom's secretary before stopping at the grocery store. I bought a loaf of bread and some fruit, grumbling that the lack of a car made it impossible to carry all I needed. The sympathetic cashier bagged my groceries and mentioned a sale at a used car sale dealer in Brownsville, a nearby town.

Returning home, I plopped the bags on my front step and fished in my purse for my key. My cell phone rang, so I stuffed the key in my jeans pocket and sat next to the grocery bags on the front step.

"Hi, Indie. You still in the office?" Peter's voice held an odd note.

"No, I just got home. Not even inside yet. Why? Did you find out about my car?"

"Well, yes and no, but that's why I'm calling. Seems there was a mix-up in the sheriff's office."

"My car?"

"The sheriff says he asked Lila to call you to pick it up if you wanted it. Lila swears she didn't hear him. The wrecking company says they received a call to haul it off, but nobody seems to know who called them."

I put a damper on my rising anger because that odd note remained in his voice. "Pete, what's going on? How could something like this happen?"

"I don't know. Lila offered to take out a loan and pay for your car, says it's all her fault."

"That's crazy. She doesn't earn much and I know she struggles to pay her bills. No, I don't want Lila to pay for the car.

She certainly wouldn't have done such a thing intentionally. Damn. Well, I guess it's time I bought a new car." I felt nauseous at the thought of my checkbook balance bottoming out at a big fat zero.

"I'm sorry, Indie."

I snorted. "It's certainly not your fault. So what's the word on the bullet holes?"

That odd note crept back into his voice. "No word yet. Listen, I gotta go. I'll be over tonight, okay?"

"Ahh, sorry, but I've got band practice again."

"I don't want you driving alone out to Steve's." A note of alarm tinged with obstinacy crept into his voice.

I fought the urge to argue by reminding myself of his kindness on the night of the storm. "I'm not. I don't *have* a car, remember? Besides, we're practicing in the basement of the community center. That way we can leave our equipment set up for the dance Friday night."

"Well, that's better." He gave his approval grudgingly. "Call you tomorrow."

I stood up, brushed the grit from the seat of my jeans and hauled my groceries into the kitchen. After putting the food away, I sat at the table, drinking coffee and trying to choose between real food and a frozen burrito heated in the microwave. The ring of my cell phone startled me. "Hello?"

"Indie, it's Steve."

"Hey, how's it going?"

"Not so good I'm afraid. We had to cancel tonight's practice."

"Why? What's going on? Are you and your family okay?" I held my breath, hoping nothing had happened to Anita or the kids.

"We're all fine." His voice rose. "It's Gerry. He's vanished."

Chapter Seven

"Oh, not again." On a scale of one to ten, my annoyance level hit a nine. "This is the third time in four months."

"I know, I know. If he doesn't show up by tomorrow, we'll have to cancel the dance gig."

"I think it's time we start looking for another bass player. Everyone who knows him has tried to help, but it hasn't done any good. Gerry's too busy feeling sorry for himself to care about anyone else, including the band." I gritted my teeth, afraid I might break out in a rant against self-pitying drunks.

"Yeah the guys and I thought it might help if he had a girlfriend. You know, help him forget about Laverne and all, but he refuses to consider it. Heck, Brady set him up with that nice girl who works at the café, but he stood her up."

"Maybe we should try one more time to get him into rehab."

"I tried and so did Anita, but he won't consider it."

"Let me know if he shows up, okay? And thanks for calling, Steve." We both knew the odds were slim that Gerry would return in time for the dance gig. His increasingly frequent disappearances were of ever-longer duration. Eventually, he would reappear, reeking of alcohol and refuse to explain his absence.

The cancellation of band practice meant I could go to bed early. After eating a bowl of vegetable soup, I dressed in my cozy flannel pajamas and fell asleep reading in bed. Something rustled in the shrubs outside my bedroom during the night, rousing me to semi-wakefulness. A blood-curdling howl erupted right under my window. "Stupid cats." I flipped off the bedside lamp and drifted back to dreamland.

Twelve hours of sleep is a gift seldom given to me. I woke refreshed and recharged, eager even for the wrangling and aggravation of dealing with a car salesman. Getting to the neighboring town without a car posed a problem. I could ask to borrow Peter's car, but how would I drive two cars back? Maybe I'd just take a cab. Since buying a car meant dipping into my savings, I might as well splurge and do it right.

Okay, that's the plan. I'll walk to the bank and transfer money from savings to checking. Then I'll take a cab to the car dealer in Brownsville.

I didn't make it to Brownsville.

One block from the bank, I glanced across the street at the offerings of our local used car lot. There it was. In the center of the lot, surrounded by faded, fluttering plastic pennants, she sat like the Queen of Cars. My dream car in my favorite car-color. A 1969 Chevy Camaro. Garnet red, white racing stripes.

I'm no car expert. Make no mistake. I don't know horsepower from a candlestick, but I'd fallen in love with the look of the 69 Camaro the first time I'd seen one cruising past. The sound of power held in abeyance, the sleek aerodynamic look. A car that could take you to the moon and back in time for dinner.

I hesitated. My plan was to purchase something inexpensive. After all, I usually walked when I needed to go somewhere around town. If I were traveling farther, I'd want something with good gas mileage. Right? Yet somehow, I found myself across the street, running a finger along the door handle and gazing at the unblemished interior.

Billy Bob Windler beamed, oozing his special brand of oily charm from every pore. "Hello, Indie. She's a beauty, isn't she? Just put her out here on the lot this morning. Sad story, really. A young, newly married man bought it in 1969. He only drove it for a few weeks before he died in accident at work. His wife didn't drive, but couldn't bear to part with it. She kept it in storage all these years, but she's decided to retire to California to be closer to her family."

"Why not take it with her?" I leaned down to peer at the odometer.

"Too expensive to ship and store. She doesn't drive, poor thing." His voice became smoother, more persuasive. "Less than five hundred miles on her. Can you believe it?"

"Pop the hood."

"Huh? Oh, yeah, sure." Billy Bob must've seen me through the window or he wouldn't have known which keys to carry with him.

I stared at the spotless engine. Unbelievable.

"Now, as you can see, she's got the Yenko transplant, you know, the 427 cubic inch V8..." His voice trailed off at a wave of my hand.

Like I would know one engine from another. I just wanted to make sure there *was* an engine. "What are you asking for it?"

He named a price that made me gasp. Huge. Irrational. Savings-destroying. My mother would throw a fit and Peter would sulk for months. I'd have almost nothing left of the money Grandfather left me. "Okay, I'll take it. Give me fifteen minutes to walk to the bank to transfer funds from savings to checking."

It was Billy Bob's turn to stare. "Just like that? Don't you even want a test drive? Uh, I mean, congratulations, Indie. You've made a fine choice. Tell you what. Take a couple of thousand off that price."

"Thanks, Billy Bob. I'll be right back, so don't sell her to anyone else."

He held out the keys. "Go on and drive to the bank. I'll have the paperwork finished by the time you get back."

Scarcely able to believe my own temporary insanity, I slid behind the wheel. The engine purred happily at the turn of the key, but I knew the hood concealed a tiger, not a kitten. I drove sedately to the bank and back, handing Billy Bob a check for such an enormous figure that I was certain to have made his Christmas card list.

My cell phone rang as I climbed back into the car.

"Indie, I'm back."

I welcomed the sound of Ruby's voice. "Hey, how was the conference or class or whatever it was?"

"Fine, fine." She paused for a moment. "We need to talk."

"About Cindy, right?"

"Yes. Listen, I'll be over there tomorrow if you have time to meet."

"How about I come to your house? I'm taking today off work and I'd like to see the kids." Driving the fifteen miles to the nearby town of Kantor where Ruby lived would give me a chance to take this beauty out on the freeway. I couldn't help grinning. "Besides, I have something to show you."

I hung up and called my insurance agent. After his gasp of shock at my switch from the VW bug to a Yenko Camaro, I gave him my credit card number to cover the increase in premiums and then, I headed out of town.

The sweetly rumbling engine nearly undid my resolve to drive within the speed limit. Without planning, I found myself tossing my hair clips on the passenger seat and rolling down the windows. *Can a woman fall in love with a car?* I laughed aloud at my ridiculous thoughts before turning to serious matters.

Cindy Brodan... What a tragedy. I wanted to wipe away the image of her lifeless body stuffed under the brush. Maybe Ruby could get more information from the sheriff than me. Surely, the bus driver would know how she ended up alone on that stormy road. If Ruby hadn't asked me to leave the investigating to the police, I'd have sought out the man.

Then there's the death of Winston Oligite—what had the police discovered about his killer? Peter hadn't mentioned it, but, to be fair, I hadn't asked. How could our sleepy little town have suffered two murders in such a short time? Especially since the most recent previous murder occurred before my birth. No, it wasn't logical. There must be a connection, but I just didn't see it.

To distract myself from these tangled thoughts, I tapped the accelerator a bit harder. Only a little, but it was enough to make my hair whirl in the breeze. I pushed my glasses up on my nose and felt like a movie star driving a fabulous car.

When I got to Ruby's house, her seven-year old son Tommy opened the door. "Wow, Mom, come see…"

I heard Tommy's five-year old sister, Amy, giggle in the living room as I held a finger to my lips. "Ssh. Don't tell. Wait for her to come to the door."

"Is that you, Indie? Come in." Ruby voice calling from the living room sounded breathless, like she'd been running.

"No, you have to come here, Mom." Tommy gave me a conspiratorial grin.

"Oh, for crying out loud. Hang on. Amy, no more wrestling. Let's go see what Auntie Indie has to show us." Ruby came to the door dressed in sweats with her hair in a ponytail. "What's so important you had to drag me from wrestling…"

"Told you, Mom. Isn't that the coolest car you ever saw? Can we go for a ride, Aunt Indie? Huh, can we?" Tommy tugged at my hand.

As elegant in sweatpants as in a business suit, Ruby waltzed out the door barefoot, Amy trailing behind her. "I don't believe it. I honestly don't believe what I'm seeing. *This* from the 'drive-'em-till-they-fall-apart' woman. The woman who saves more than she spends. The woman who—"

"Okay, okay. I get the idea. So, what do you think?" I laughed and gestured toward the car.

They crowded around the Camaro, peering through the windows and exclaiming over the beautiful red color. Even Ruby's husband, Mark, joined the appreciative throng. He sighed with regret when invited to come along for a ride. "Thanks, Indie. I'd love to, but I have to go back to work. Another catastrophic computer failure. Have fun and see all of you later." He kissed Ruby on the cheek, ruffled Tommy's hair and hugged Amy. With a wave goodbye, he climbed into his car and left.

"Okay, how about ice cream for all? Who wants a ride to the ice cream store?" I loved taking Tommy and Amy to the local ice cream shop and did so every chance I got. They had fun, but I think I enjoyed myself even more watching them deliberate flavor choices.

Amy hugged her brother in excitement. "Ice cream!"

Tommy's eyes gleamed and he asked, "In your car, Aunt Indie?"

I smiled at the two equally adorable children. They looked more like twins every time I saw them, despite their disparate sizes. Both blond and blue-eyed with sweet dispositions. Tommy had grown quite tall for his years, while Amy remained petite for hers. "Of course in my car. All aboard."

After buckling the children into their seat belts, Ruby climbed into the passenger seat and spoke in a low voice, "We need to speak later. Can you spend the night?"

"I didn't bring overnights things. No toothbrush, no pajamas."

"Don't be silly. You know I've got stuff you can borrow."

"Make it go fast, Aunt Indie." Tommy patted the seat with a grin.

"Uh, I don't think your mother would appreciate me driving like a wild woman with you two in the car." I laughed and glanced over at Ruby. From the set of her jaw and the troubled look on her face, I guessed that she'd learned of poor Cindy's fate. "Okay, I'll stay the night and we can talk later, but right now there's a double-scoop with my name on it."

The ice cream store proved a hit. After scoops of assorted flavors with sprinkles and lots of laughter, even the worry lines softened on Ruby's forehead. We walked outside into the late afternoon sunshine where the Camaro immediately drew my gaze. *Ah, how I love red cars.* I smiled at my own silliness. "How about a trip to the park?"

Amy jumped up and down, her pigtails bouncing and a smudge of chocolate ice cream on her cheek. "Yes, yes! Can we, Mommy?"

"Can Aunt Indie make the car go fast this time? Please?" Tommy's gaze, like mine, locked on the car the moment we had stepped through the door onto the sidewalk.

Ruby grinned at her son. "Not a chance, Mister. I hate to put a damper on this party, but I've got to start dinner or these two won't get to bed on time."

Both children groaned and exchanged doleful expressions.

"How about if we drop you off at the house to start dinner and I take the kids to the park for half an hour?"

"Please, Mommy?" Amy gazed with those irresistible baby-blues at her mother.

Tommy tried a slightly more adult approach. "We don't get to see Aunt Indie very often, Mom."

Ruby laughed and conceded defeat. "Okay, but half an hour only. Then it's home for dinner, baths and straight to bed."

We dropped off Ruby at the house, where before departing I took the opportunity to rev the engine to the children's delight and their mother's mock chagrin. After driving the few minutes to the park, I chose a spot near the playground equipment and helped Amy take off her seatbelt.

The setting sun provided a perfect backdrop to the lovely park. Stately oak trees ringed the play area and flowering shrubs scented the air. Water gurgled in a majestic fountain resting in the center of the well-manicured lawn. Despite the lateness of the day, children crowded the playground equipment while adults watched indulgently from wooden benches. Tommy and Amy ran off to join friends and I settled myself to supervise.

Bits of the other parents' conversations drifted my way.

"The kids are spending the weekend with Grandma. Romantic weekend in the cabin…"

"No, my sister did it. She said…"

"Can you believe how tall Billy is? That boy…"

"I heard he disappeared right from this park. Not two days ago."

I perked up from my almost-doze. Tommy and Amy played with their friends, not ten feet away while the other parents continued to chat.

"I don't believe it. We'd have heard something. If it's true, why hasn't it been on the news?"

"It's true. I was here right after it happened. No idea why it's being hushed up…"

The two women rose from the nearby bench and left the park, leaving me wondering about their conversation. A sudden wave of dread washed over me, a premonition. The hair on my arms stood up and my mouth felt suddenly dry. I jumped to my feet and gazed wildly around. *Calm yourself, you idiot. See? Amy is on the swing and Tommy is right…where's Tommy?*

"Aunt Indie, can you help me? My shoelace is untied, but there's a knot and I can't fix it." Tommy tugged at my sleeve.

"Of course, sweetie." Relieved, I knelt and tackled the offending knot. "There you go."

Tommy scampered off to join his friends on the merry-go-round while my eyes automatically searched for Amy. It took a minute for me to register what I saw, or rather, didn't see.

Amy had disappeared.

Chapter Eight

Filled with an indescribable dread and terror, I whirled around and around, searching for a flash of blond pigtails. *My God, she was just here. There was no adult closer than the benches, nobody on the swings except children.* "Tommy, where's Amy?"

Tommy halted his headlong rush to the teeter-totter, swiveling his head from the swings to me, a puzzled expression on his cherubic face. "Huh? I just saw her on the swing."

I grabbed his arm, unwilling to let him out of my sight, and dragged him with me to the nearest bench. "Excuse me, but have you seen a little blond girl? Five years old, small for her age, pigtails, pink dress."

"No, I'm sorry." The two women looked startled. "Your child is missing?"

Too panicked for polite discussions, I simply nodded and headed for the swings where I'd last seen Amy. Maybe I'd just missed her. *That must be it. I just didn't see her in the group of little girls. Okay, calm down. Calm down. Try looking again.* The noise of my own heart pounding in my ears nearly deafened me.

Thus, I missed the faint giggle emanating from behind a nearby tree. Thankfully, Tommy's younger and less concerned ears heard it. With a look of disgust, he grabbed my hand and dragged me toward several lilac shrubs, their leaves glossy in the setting sun. "I think she's over there, Aunt Indie."

My stomach churned and my mouth felt so dry that I couldn't speak. I knelt on the ground and peered through the lilacs while continuing to clutch Tommy's sleeve. There she sat amidst the shrubs and assorted bits of wind-blown detritus, one hand covering her wide smile and muffling her giggles while the other hand picked twigs from her dress.

I brushed aside a cola can, scraps of paper, a broken guitar pick and a deflated basketball. Kneeling in the cleared space, I grasped her arm and tugged her from the brush.

Relief flooded through me, followed by quickly stifled anger. *How could she play a trick like that? Doesn't she know how frightening it is to lose a child?* Sudden realization smacked me right in my bone-headed face. *Of course she doesn't understand, you idiot. She's five years old.*

Tommy stared at his sister. "Amy, Mommy told you not to hide anymore. Remember when you hid in the closet and she couldn't find you? You had to go to bed early."

Amy's eyes widened and she scrambled out of the bushes in such a hurry that she snagged the hem of her dress. *Sccritchhh.* Ignoring the torn hem, I marched both children to the Camaro. After fastening their seat belts, I locked the doors and sat in the driver's seat, my hands trembling and my knees knocking together under the steering wheel.

"Can we go home now? I'm hungry." Tommy's voice held that plaintive feed-me note I'd noticed in other friends' young children.

The jingle of keys as I reached for the ignition almost obscured Amy's whispered words.

"That man was a bad stranger."

I felt faint as I turned in my seat to look at her. The solemn expression on her face did nothing to assuage my fears. "What man, honey?"

Amy pulled her thumb from her mouth with a pop. "That bad stranger by the tree. He said I had to come with him."

I could barely breathe. *My God, had I truly come so close to losing her? I only looked away for a minute to fix Tommy's shoelace. How can parents wake every morning knowing such horror, such evil, exists?* "Can you tell me what the man looked like, Amy?"

She shook her head. "He had a big hat. I told him I wasn't allowed to talk to strangers."

"Was he tall or short? Old or young?" *How can I tell Ruby that I nearly lost her daughter? How can I face Mark?*

Amy twitched the folds of her dress and stared at her lap, not meeting my eyes.

"It's okay, honey. We're going home now. We'll talk about it later."

"But Aunt Indie, I told him 'stranger danger' and I crawled under the bushes so he couldn't reach me." With an air of innocent triumph, Amy poked her thumb back in her mouth.

I drove slowly to Ruby's house, my hands shaking all the way.

****

After bedtime stories, teddy bear kisses and window locks double-checked, the children slept tucked under their blankets. Mark snored from the master bedroom while Ruby and I sat in the living room with cups of coffee. She tried to console me. "Indie, you did nothing wrong. The incident terrifies me, but you're placing blame in the wrong place."

"Wrong or not, Tommy and Amy were my responsibility. When I think of what might have happened…" I felt tears welling up again for the bazillionth time since returning to the house. "Wait a minute. I remember hearing a conversation at the park about a missing child. Did you hear of a boy disappearing last week?"

"Nooo," drawled Ruby with a frown, "but I certainly should have, if it's true. It should have been on the news and in the papers."

"Maybe she was mistaken, but she sounded so sure. In fact, she said she was there right after it happened."

"I think I'll give the chief of police a call tomorrow. Ask if it's true and if so, maybe I can find out why the information hasn't been released."

"Yeah, you'd think they'd want to warn parents to be on the look-out. People might even want to avoid the park until they catch the guy if the story is true." I tried to stifle a yawn. Without success, I might add.

"Come on, time for bed. We could both use some sleep. If I can sleep through Mark's snores." She nodded her head toward the bedroom.

I lay awake for a long time, thinking about what might have happened. If Ruby and Mark hadn't taught Amy how to respond to strangers. If Amy hadn't crawled far enough back into the shrubs where an adult couldn't reach. If I'd taken longer to notice her missing. If, if, if.

Something niggled and gnawed at my brain, something I couldn't quite name. I had that warning bell feeling, but it took its time finding its way to the surface. It leaked slowly, slowly into my consciousness, like air leaking out of an old balloon. Only in reverse.

Our quiet little area of the state had lost its glow of peace and harmony. First, Winston Oligite and then Cindy Brodan. Now, thirty miles away from my house, a stranger tried to abduct Amy. The hair on my arms stood up and I tried to dissuade myself from my current train of thought.

I saw no strange man in the park. Maybe it was Amy's imagination, part of some silly childhood game, but she wasn't a fanciful child. Giggly at times, yes, but not fanciful. And there was nothing imaginary or fanciful about murder. Two murders.

I drifted into a doze, worn out by the day's drama, but sat bolt upright a few moments later. It wasn't just the murders and the possible abduction that bothered me. It was my own mindset. I'd fallen into a dull work routine of passive investigation. Waiting for reports from the sheriff, waiting to read files, waiting for the Clerk of Court office to open so I could dig through index cards.

I was a private investigator, dammit. It was time I started making use of my P.I. license, do some real work and find some real answers. Sheriff Muley would find me in his face if I didn't get answers about Cindy's autopsy and by God, I wanted to know about Winston's death, too. Time for some real sleuthing.

With that out of the way, I fell into an uneasy slumber filled with dreams of running through the park, calling out Amy's name.

****

I headed home the next morning, the purr of the Camaro soothing my nerves until I remembered something else. In the excitement of buying a new car, I'd forgotten to call Peter. More interesting, Peter hadn't called me.

Since we first developed a serious relationship, he'd wanted to know everything about me. He insisted on knowing where I went, what I did, what I bought, what I ate. At first, I'd thought it a sweet expression of his concern and fondness for me, but it soon became a frustrating battle of wills. I genuinely cared about him, maybe even loved him, but I had tired quickly of his urge to control and we now argued on a daily basis.

Controlling a childish urge to stick out my tongue at the sight of his name in my phone's contact list, I pulled off the road and dialed his cell number. No answer. *Hmm, probably asleep or at work and can't answer.* I tossed my phone onto the passenger seat and drove home.

After a shower and a cup of coffee, I tried Peter's number again. Still no answer. This time I left a voice message telling him to call me. I wasn't worried about him, but did feel a bit uneasy. Very unusual not to hear from him. Ah, well, maybe I'd run into him during the day.

I filled my travel mug with fresh, hot coffee and grabbed my car keys, pausing in the doorway to admire the Camaro. *Damn, she's a beauty.* I admired her all the way to the sheriff's office. Time for a showdown with Muley.

"Okay, I'm here on behalf of Ruby Langdon and I'd like a copy of the coroner's report on Cindy Brodan."

Sheriff Muley narrowed his eyes and glared at me. "You got something official that shows me you're working for Langdon?" He poured over the signed and notarized statement from Ruby, occasionally looking up to glare at me while neglecting to offer me a seat.

"Well?" I tried to hide my annoyance.

"Well," he drawled. "The way I see it, this piece of paper don't do you no good, Missy."

"What the hell are you talking about, Muley?"

"Cindy Brodan is dead, so Ruby Langdon has no client." He handed back my document and leaned back in his chair, ostentatiously putting his feet on the desk.

"Fine." I refused to let him see how much he irritated me. "See you at the next Commissioners meeting."

"Huh, what?" The booted feet hit the floor with a thump.

"I intend to lodge a formal complaint about the destruction of my car." I gave him a sweet smile and sashayed out the door.

Once in the Camaro, I phoned Ruby and gave her the news.

"Damn. I didn't think Muley would even realize the connection between Cindy's death and the end of the attorney-client relationship." Ruby sounded as aggravated with the sheriff as I felt.

"Muley has never seemed like much of a thinker. I'm betting he got his info from someone else."

"Who? And why would he even be asking someone about it?"

"I don't know, but I'm starting to feel that something's going on and we're the only ones who know nothing about it."

"Oh, don't get all conspiracy-theorist on me." Ruby laughed. "Next, you'll be talking about the Roswell aliens."

"Well, it wouldn't surprise me if Muley's an alien from some planet where they have rocks for brains."

"Tsk, tsk. I think you need a little vacation. You're sounding grumpy."

"I know, I know. All the weird stuff going on is getting to me."

"Me, too." Ruby's voice turned serious. "Lots of scary stuff. I want you to promise that you won't do anything stupid."

"Me? Do something stupid? You know better than that."

"I mean it, Indie. There's at least one killer loose."

"I won't forget."

I sat in the car after we'd hung up, trying Peter's cell phone. Still no answer. Again, I left a message for him to call me and then, against all logic, I headed out of town to the location where I'd found Cindy.

With the crime scene tape removed and the ground churned up by booted law enforcement officials, little remained to identify the bushes where the killer had hidden the body. I searched for half an hour with goosebumps raising the hair on my arms. The storm left its own scars on the area—fallen trees, shrubs buried in mud, dead birds.

At last, I located the bushes and scoured the immediate area for anything the sheriff and his deputies might have missed. I found nothing but bad memories. The vision of poor Cindy's body lying alone under a bush refused to leave my mind. Did she die here or did her killer murder her elsewhere and then, dump her body here?

What a tragedy for her family. Maybe I'd visit and offer condolences. *Time to leave this creepy place anyway.* An eerie silence enveloped me, as if every bird and cricket had left for another part of the world. Suddenly, I couldn't wait to get back to my car. I ran.

Stop being stupid. There's nothing frightening here.

I forced myself to slow to a walk and it's a good thing I did or I'd have missed the tiny glint of something metallic. It was a badge, buried in the now dry mud. Only the minutest corner visible in the deep boot prints. Using a twig, I pried it up.

Some dumbass lost his badge when they carried out Cindy's body. Well, I'd give it to Peter and let him return it. The thought of Peter reminded me that I'd left my phone in the Camaro. Damn. Better hustle back. I might have missed a call from him.

I trudged back to the car, ignoring the goosebumps on my arms and forcing myself to walk at a slow pace. What a relief to get into the car, toss the mud-encrusted badge on the passenger side floor and lock the doors. I stuck the key in the ignition before remembering I needed to check my voice mail. Nothing from Peter, but one message from Steve. "Indie, call me as soon as you get this. It's important."

The Camaro roared back to town, my determination to drive within the speed limit becoming feebler each time I climbed behind the wheel. What a joy to drive! I parked at the bus station and patted the seat before getting out. *I should've bought one of these years ago.*

"Can I help you?" The girl, barely out of her teens, spoke without taking her eyes from the tiny television set in the corner. She chewed her gum with loud smacking sounds and twisted her blond hair around her finger.

"Yes, I'd like the name of the driver on the night run of Route 241 a week ago."

"Um, can you come back? Like in half an hour. I'm just answering the phone for Rose. She went to lunch."

The girl's eyes never left the television. I pointed to a bulletin hanging on the rear wall beside a cluttered desk. "There's a work schedule on the bulletin board. You can get the driver's name from it."

"Um, I don't know. Can you wait for Rose?"

I slapped the chipped, Formica countertop with just enough force to get the girl's attention. Startled, she turned to look at me. She was younger than I'd thought, maybe thirteen or fourteen, with big, blue eyes nearly obscured by over-long bangs. Blue jeans, t-shirt and dangly earrings.

Young enough for me to try a bit of bluster. "I can't wait. I work for an attorney and I need information. Now, will you give me the driver's name or do I need to return with a court order?" Guilt washed over me at the deception, but I clung to the hope of learning something about Cindy's killer.

The girl's eyes widened and her voice developed a whiny tone. "A court order? I don't know how to tell who was driving. Rose will be back soon."

"Hand me the schedule and I'll look myself." Doing my best to appear official, I scanned the schedule and quickly typed driver's name and phone number into my phone's notepad app. "Thank you for your cooperation." I scrammed before the return of the redoubtable Rose, who I suspected would not cave to empty threats.

When I phoned the driver, Manny Olson, he agreed to see me. My beautiful Camaro took me the fourteen miles to #14 Hedgerow Drive, Ellertown in record time.

"Come in, come in." With a sweep of his arm, Manny welcomed me into his home. Mid-sixties, average height, slight paunch, brilliant green eyes and thinning, gray hair that he continually brushed back from his face, Manny proved pleasant and willing, but ultimately unhelpful.

"Mr. Olson, please tell me what you remember of Cindy Brodan, the young girl who rode your bus." I sipped from the huge mug of coffee he kindly offered. Good stuff.

"Please, call me Manny."

"Okay, Manny, please tell me what you know."

"Yes, well, as I told you when you called, I don't know much. The girl got on the bus alone in Brushwalla. I noticed her because she seemed too young to travel alone, but her ticket was in order."

"Did you speak with her?"

"Only when she handed me her ticket. Said she'd been visiting an aunt and was on her way home."

"How did she seem? Was she frightened? Maybe happy to be going home?"

He shrugged. "Like I said, we really didn't talk much, but she seemed okay. Maybe a little tired, but fine. I'm sorry. I wish I could be of more help."

"You're doing great and I appreciate you taking the time to see me. Now, did you make any stops on that route?"

"Just one. It's a scheduled stop at that gas station halfway between Deemouth and Ellertown."

"Do your riders get off the bus there?"

"Normally, no. There's nothing there but the gas station. No amenities. The girl got off the bus, though, to make a phone call. Reason I remember is that she was the only one who got off there. Long time since anyone got off there." He brushed back his hair and sniffed. "It's dirty. Nobody keeps it up, you know. My riders are mostly regulars who know that, so they seldom even use the restroom."

"Who did she call?"

"I'm sorry, but I don't know. I was busy signing the receipt for the fuel and by the time I'd finished, she was back in her seat."

"Okay, so she called someone and then got off the bus several miles out of Oakdale. Why did she get off the bus so far out of town? That's not one of your usual stops, is it?"

"No, of course it isn't a usual stop. I tried to tell the girl the route ended in town and I couldn't just stop the bus in the middle of the road. She seemed very agitated and begged me to let her off, said her friend was picking her up there and she wouldn't have a ride home if I didn't stop the bus." He brushed back the thinning hair again and looked at me with sorrowful eyes. "If I hadn't let her off the bus, she'd still be alive, wouldn't she? That poor little girl."

"Manny, this wasn't your fault. I'm going to find the person who did this." My resolve hardened at the look of guilt and sorrow on his kind face. "One more question. Did you see this friend of Cindy's? Did you see anyone?"

He shook his head, dislodging his hair and brushing it from his face again. "No, I saw no one. I thought I glimpsed a white vehicle behind the trees off the road, but I'm not sure. I was too worried about getting into trouble for making an unscheduled stop to pay attention."

"Okay, thank you for your time. And thanks for the coffee." I shook his hand and stepped outside, but turned back when a thought occurred to me. "One more thing. Which side of the road did you see the flash of white?"

"Hm, let me think." He rubbed his chin, thinking aloud. "I opened the door for the girl. Of course, we were heading north and the door opened to the east side of the road. It would've been the left side where I saw the white, whatever it was. So, yes, the west. It would've been the west side of the road into Lintown."

After thanking him again, I hopped into the Camaro with the intention of driving straight home for a shower, but an impulsive desire to check Manny's story overwhelmed me. I parked the car beside the road across from the bushes where I'd found Cindy.

Once again, the place creeped me out. I deliberately faced away from the side of the road where I'd parked on that stormy night. Still, the hair on my arms stood up and my mouth filled with a metallic taste. *You're being ridiculous. Maybe you need to bring a picnic lunch and sit out here for an afternoon and prove to yourself that there's nothing to fear. Don't let the wicked win.*

Manny told the truth. It took only moments to find tire tracks just behind the tree line where an old dirt road led deeper into the forest. The road crossed onto private property not far back and nobody had used it in years. Despite the battering by the storm, recent tire tracks stood out in stark relief against the old track.

With one hand clinging to the cell phone in my pocket for courage, I tiptoed between trees to find the spot where the mysterious car had parked. I found boot prints heading toward the spot, but none leading away. *He, or she, must have been here before the storm began and all that water washed away his tracks. Maybe this is where he, or she, killed Cindy. But, why would you move the body? This area is isolated and unpopulated. Nobody would've found her, not for years.*

Shivering despite the warm afternoon temperature, I trekked toward the car, so absorbed in my thoughts that I nearly missed the metallic glint of the spent shell casing. *Here. Whoever shot at me must've stood here.* I peered through the trees, envisioning my old Bug parked beside the road. No, it wouldn't work. No way could the shooter see the road from this spot.

Besides, I'd clearly heard more than one shot and I knew the Bug had several bullet holes, but I saw only one casing.

Careful not to disturb evidence, I knelt to look closely at the empty casing, expecting to find additional shells, but I discovered something far more unsettling.

A pair of panties lay less than three feet away from the spent shell casing.

Chapter Nine

Time to call the police. *Hang on…the bullet holes in my car were evidence, proof that someone tried to kill me, but my car disappeared into a crusher machine. Was it deliberate or the result of incompetence? Probably the latter, but still…*I pulled out my cell phone and dialed Peter's number. No answer, so I left a voice message stressing the word 'urgent.'

I couldn't stand here all day waiting for a phone call. *How to mark the spot?* With sudden inspiration, I yanked up a clump of wildflowers and then, broke off an evergreen branch, leaving a sharp stub. I impaled the flowers, dirt and all, on the tree trunk. Nobody could mistake that bright flash of color for a natural growth on a tree.

The scent of pine and wildflowers filled the air, imparting the disorienting impression of Christmas in a tropical clime. Dirt and tree sap stained my hands. I tried to remove it by rubbing my palms on my jeans, but succeeded only in spreading the mess to my clothes. Shrugging with resignation at my usual untidy state, I checked my phone to make sure the ringer was on and then, headed closer to the road to search for the likely hiding spot of the shooter.

The underbrush grew thicker as I neared the road. I shoved my way through it, looking for a spot where I could see my car, yet remain hidden from anyone on the road. After half an hour, I had found nothing. Bits of twig and bark clung to my jeans. One of my hair clips had fallen out and I'd scraped my elbow.

You look a mess, dearie. Time to give it up and let the big boys come do their job. I snorted. *Yeah, the big boys who'd managed to send bullet hole evidence through the crusher.*

Just before stepping out onto the shoulder of the road, I glanced down and there it was. Evidence that someone had stood or knelt here, taking shots at me. Half a dozen shell casings clustered in a small circle. The dull metal gleamed in the afternoon sun and before I realized what I was doing, I'd pulled a tissue out of my pocket and picked one up.

You know better than to touch crime scene evidence. All the same, I carried the casing to my car and tucked it into a separate pocket of my purse, which I'd stuffed under the driver's seat before traipsing into the woods. *Oh, my God, I don't believe I did that. Ruby will wring my neck and Peter…I don't want to think about what he'll say.*

I drove home, still in a quandary over calling the sheriff. After the episode this morning, I dreaded the thought of Muley's reaction when I told him I'd sought out a crime scene. No, I'd wait for Peter to return my call so I could report to him. The shell casings had lain there for days and there was no reason they would disappear.

A shower. That's what I needed. With half my hair hanging in my face for lack of a hair clip and my clothes covered with dirt and pinesap, it was hard to think straight. Yep, a shower would clear my brain. I left the Camaro in the driveway and unlocked the front door.

A loud snore greeted me. Peter slept sprawled on my couch, one arm across his face and the other drooping onto the floor. His uniform looked rumpled and his hair unwashed. *Wow, I guess he's been working long hours or he'd never allow himself to look so un-groomed. He looks kinda sweet, though. Maybe if I tiptoe past him, I can take a shower before he wakes up and sees me so filthy.*

I made it as far as the bathroom door.

"Indie? Is that you?" Peter groaned and when I turned back, I saw him struggling to sit up.

"Hey, big guy. Long time no see." I plopped down beside him and stretched to kiss his cheek. "Boy, you look like you haven't slept in a week."

He reached out to ruffle my hair before leaning back and closing his eyes. "Maybe more than a week."

"Why? What's going on? I've left messages for you to call me."

"I know, I know. I'm sorry, but I couldn't. Been working on something important and couldn't stop."

"Wow, what's so important that you couldn't stop to sleep?" The closer I looked at him, the worse he looked. The circles under his eyes were so dark he looked like a raccoon and his uniform…well, it was, frankly, downright *fragrant.* A sense of alarm swept over me. "Peter, what is it? What's going on?"

He waved a hand in a vague circle without opening his eyes. "Nothing, at least nothing I can talk about it. I need to sleep before we talk, okay?"

"Yeah, sure, you poor guy. Here, let me help you to bed." I bit my lip. The crime scene discovery would have to wait. I tugged him to his feet and draped his arm over my shoulder. Even with my support, he barely made it the ten feet to the bedroom. He snored as I pulled off his boots and covered him with a blanket.

After showering, I spent the next few hours pacing barefoot around the house. I drank coffee and tried to read, but couldn't seem to sit still. Calling Ruby was out; talking might wake Peter. Same with practicing my violin. I wandered outside and sat on the front step, sipping from my mug.

Why do I feel so reluctant to tell Muley what I found? Is it because I don't like him? I didn't really believe that was the reason. Professional people often worked with others they detested. It was part of being a professional. *Do I believe Muley is crooked? He* did *send my car to the crusher, destroying evidence that someone shot at me.* I snorted. *More likely, he's just a dumbass.*

Peter awoke after I'd had enough coffee to float a large ship. He came stumbling, red-eyed, out of the bedroom. "Hey, good-looking, got another cup of that stuff?"

"Sure thing. Have a seat." I made a cup of coffee as he parked himself at the kitchen table. "So, what's been keeping you so busy?"

"Just work. You know. The usual stuff." He waved a hand. "What about you? I've missed you, you know."

"Well, I spent a night at Ruby's. Just girl talk stuff. Mark had to work late."

"Hmm. How are the kids?" He sat his cup on the table and rubbed his eyes. "I need a shower. Then another cup of coffee, okay?"

"Sure, but Peter, there's something I need to tell you."

"Shower first, okay? I need to shock my brain awake."

He came out of the shower smelling cleaner and wearing a pair of old sweats that he kept in my closet. "Ah, better. Do I smell eggs?"

"Yep." I sat a plate heaped with scrambled eggs and toast in front of him.

"Thanks, Indie. Now what did you want to tell me?" He shoveled eggs into his mouth as if he hadn't eaten in a month.

I told him about finding the panties and a nearby shell casing. "Right off the road, behind a tree, I found another spot with half a dozen empty shells. Definitely the spot where the shooter stood taking pot shots at me."

He stared at me. "Have you called the sheriff?"

"No, not yet. I wanted to tell you."

"Let's go."

"What? Don't you need to call this in or something?" I watched as he stuffed the last bit of toast in his mouth and stood up.

"Later, after we get there."

"Okay, let me clean up this mess."

"No, let's leave now. I'll help you clean up later." He dashed into the bedroom and came out with his old tennis shoes and a blue duffle bag holding his dirty uniform. "We'll have to call a cab to take us to my apartment to get my car. My squad car isn't here. I had a friend drop me off."

Why hadn't I realized his car wasn't here? "Uh, there's something else I need to tell you." I had hoped to break the news to him later, slowly.

He finished tying his shoes and stood up. "What's that? Can it wait until I call a cab?"

"You don't need to call a cab."

"What?" He flipped his phone shut and waited.

I opened the front door and gestured toward the driveway.

"Wow, where'd you borrow something like that?" He cast an admiring glance at the garnet red Camaro gleaming in the late afternoon sunshine.

"I didn't borrow it. I bought it."

"You WHAT?" He turned back to me, admiration replaced by fury.

"Yep, I bought it from Billy Bob. She's a beauty, isn't she?"

He stomped back into the house, dragging me with him. "How could you do something like that without asking me? It must have cost a fortune."

I jerked my sleeve from his grasp. "Actually, it's none of your business how much it cost and why would I need to ask you before I spend *my* money?"

"Your money? I thought we were a team. We're supposed to share decisions like this. You have no right to do something like this without asking me first."

Despite my determination to remain calm, my face grew hot and I heard the irritation in my voice. "A team? Peter, you're my *boyfriend*. Not my father and certainly not my husband. Did you ask me before you bought that expensive truck of yours? No and there's no reason you should have asked me."

"Take it back. You take that car back as soon as we've had a look at whatever you found. I'll call one of the guys to give us a ride to my house from Billy Bob's place." He glared at me.

I stared at him in disbelief. Giving him slack because he needed sleep was one thing, but this was too much. "I will *not* take it back. I bought this with money left to me by my grandfather. *My* earnings from *my* job take care of the insurance and maintenance."

His eyes widened and his mouth opened. I forestalled the tirade by stepping out the door onto the front step. "Let's go. Discussion over."

"Oh, this discussion is far from over, but it makes me wonder if something else isn't over." He shoved past me to the driver's side door and stopped, holding out a hand.

As I dug in my purse for the keys, a feeling of resolve grew in my chest. *No, not again. I'm not giving in to bad behavior to avoid an argument.* I ignored the outstretched palm, unlocked the driver's side door and climbed in behind the steering wheel. When he got into the passenger seat and slammed the door with sufficient force to rattle my bones, I gritted my teeth and said nothing.

Not a word passed between us during the disquieting drive. Peter sat as if someone had glued the tip of his nose to the side window. I saw nothing but the back of his head, his black hair still damp from the shower.

"Here we are." I pulled off the road, stuffed my purse under the seat and hopped out of the car.

Peter joined me, still not speaking, and gestured for me to lead the way.

I pointed to the clump of flowers impaled on the tree branch, the blooms long since wilted. "There was nothing else to mark the spot."

The corners of Peter's mouth curled up in an almost-grin before he set his jaw and turned away. He shook his head when he spotted the panties lying nearly buried in mud and pine needles. "Okay, I need to radio the office to get a team out here. Show me where the shooter stood beside the road. After that, you can leave. I'm sure Sheriff Muley will want to talk to you later at the office about how you found the place."

Shivering at the coldness in his voice, but still angry enough to ignore it, I clambered through the brush to the spot where I'd found the shells. Nothing. Zip. Nada.

"You sure this is the right place?" He didn't look at me, but continued to walk around the area gazing down carefully before each step.

"Yes, I'm sure." I rubbed my arms, trying to still a sudden frisson. *What if I'd been here when this person showed up to remove the spent shells?* "It's only been a few hours since I was here. I wish I'd thought to take a picture with my cell phone camera."

"Not your fault, Indie. Go on. Go home. I'll call you later to let you know when the sheriff wants to talk to you. Damn, damn, damn. I wish they'd missed at least one empty shell." He glanced at his watch and spoke absently, not really looking at me. Squatting beside a scuffed area, he was peering under the brush.

"Uh, Peter, there's something I should probably give to you."

"Yeah? What's that?" He continued to crawl on his knees, scrutinizing the ground under every bush.

"I'm only going to show you if you promise not to lecture me."

That got his attention and he straightened, staring at me with those green eyes. "What is it, Indie? What do you have?"

"Just a minute." I ran back to the car for my purse.

He watched and waited for me to catch my breath.

I opened my purse and pulled out the spent casing, still wrapped in its tissue cocoon.

His eyes widened. "You removed evidence from the scene of the crime?"

"Honestly, I don't know what made me do it. There were so many of them and before I knew what I was doing, I scooped one up and put it in my purse." I looked at the ground, unable to meet his eyes.

"You realize you could lose your investigator's license for this?" His gaze was relentless, cold.

"Yes, I'm sorry. I do know better."

"Well, it can't be used as evidence because the chain of custody has been disturbed, but it may be useful. Did you touch this with your bare hands?"

I shook my head. "No, I picked it up with the tissue."

"Okay, but you know I have to report this. There may be repercussions for you. Now, go. Go home, Indie."

"You want me to just leave you here? Without any way to get to town?"

"Yes, yes. Just go. I've got back up on the way."

"What about your duffle bag? You want me to drop it by your place later?"

"Huh? No, don't bother. Just sit it on the ground and I'll grab it when I leave." He didn't look at me as I left.

I glanced back several times, but he hadn't moved from his squat by the time I reached the Camaro. As I drove away leaving the blue bag sitting beside the road, I had a feeling that this was both a beginning and an end.

The purr of the engine soothed something in my soul as I drove back to town and the quiet drive settled my nerves. There wasn't much traffic, although I did wave to Anita, Steve's wife, as she drove by in her clunky station wagon. A deputy sheriff car from another county, a big blue pickup truck and a small foreign sports car. A quiet part of the world, Oakdale.

At home, I parked the Camaro in the driveway, planning to change into clean clothes and call Ruby before I went to the office. Dressed in clean jeans and a white blouse, I settled in at the kitchen table with a steaming cup of coffee and picked up my phone.

A sudden blast of Beethoven startled me as the phone rang before I could punch in Ruby's number. Hot coffee sloshed over the edge of the cup onto my hand and the table. I wiped my hands on my clean jeans and shook my head at the stain spreading over the white tablecloth.

"Hello."

"Indie? This is Steve."

"Hey, Steve. How's it going? Any word from our errant bass player?"

"Uh, that's what I'm calling about."

I waited for him to continue, but he didn't. "Well? What happened this time? Which sleazy dive did you find him in now?"

In a voice so low that I could barely hear him, Steve said, "Indie, he wasn't in one of his usual haunts."

"Okay, what gives? What's the big mystery? Oh, damn, he's in jail again, isn't he?" *That stupid bastard. What family venue is going to keep hiring a band with a member who's been in jail umpteen times for dui and bar brawling?*

"No, he isn't in jail."

"Steve, I don't mean to be rude, but I need to get to the office. I have work to do. You wanna just tell me where he is and I'll see what I can do, okay?"

"There's nothing you can do. Not you or anyone else."

I gritted my teeth, trying to quell my irritation. "Well?"

"He's in the morgue." The words came out as if forced. "Gerry's dead."

"What?" The air whooshed out of my lungs. I felt like someone had punched me in the chest. Hard.

"Somebody blew his head off. Sheriff said it was a burglary gone wrong." His voice broke.

"Where did this happen? When?"

"I don't know. Listen, Indie, I need to go. Anita needs me for something right now. I'll call you later, okay?"

I sat my phone on the table with a feeling that the world whirled out of control. Crazy thoughts spun in circles, round and round, but one idea stayed put. Little Oakdale, our quiet and peaceful town, harbored a crazed killer.

Chapter Ten

Muley himself answered the phone when I called the sheriff's department. "I'm sorry, Indie, but you know I can't release that information."

"Look, I'm only asking to know what happened."

"No information will be released until the next of kin have been notified."

"Dammit, he *has* no next of kin, no family and you *know* that, Muley."

"Sorry, Indie, but rules is rules."

The satisfaction in his voice made me want to reach through the phone and strangle him. "Yes, rules *are* rules. Therefore, please inform me in advance when you wish to speak to me about the crime scene I discovered. I'll want my attorney present."

He spluttered into the phone and I imagined his face growing red. "Now, hang on a minute. There's no need to get all formal on me. You're not a suspect or anything."

"That's good to know. Don't forget; call Ruby Langdon to schedule an appointment for questioning." Okay, so I knew the whole thing was ridiculous, but I admit I relished obstructing Muley's power trip. My face stretched in a wide grin, although I tried to keep my enjoyment out of my voice. "See ya, Muley."

He roared as I disconnected and I hoped he wasn't exorcizing his pique on an innocent employee, like Lila May. I'd already forgiven her the faux pas of sending my car to the crusher. After all, the loss of the Bug led me to the Camaro and besides, I still wasn't convinced Muley himself hadn't ordered the car destroyed.

Ruby answered her phone on the first ring. "I thought I'd be hearing from you. I heard through the grapevine that somebody found Gerry. What happened?"

I explained my abortive attempt to garner information. "So you can expect a call from the sheriff's office. I'd better warn you that I ticked off Muley by insisting that my attorney be present."

"That wasn't smart, Indie. Something's going on and I think you'd be safer if you didn't make an enemy of everyone on the right side of the law." I heard the frown in her voice, even though I couldn't see her face.

"I'm not too worried about it. Muley's a big jerk and you know it. Besides, it's getting harder to tell who is on the right side of the law." Even I knew I sounded petulant. All the weird stuff was beginning to get on my nerves.

"Yes, I know, but still…"

"Gerry has no family and Muley knows that. He's just being stubborn."

"Of course he is, but all the same, Indie. I sure would like to get a peek at the ballistics report."

"Are you sure Gerry was shot? That's what Steve said, but I wasn't sure he knew."

"Yes. At least that's what I heard. I guess Steve filed a missing persons report and eventually one of Muley's deputies went to Gerry's house. Nobody answered the door, so the deputy kicked it open. Found Gerry dead, shot in the back. They are saying he must've come home and surprised a burglar. Lots of stuff missing. Guns, stereo equipment, computer. Expensive stuff."

"So somebody broke in, shot Gerry and then, stopped to lock the door when he, or she, left?"

"I know, I know. I wondered that myself, but who knows? Stranger things have happened."

"Especially lately. I'm thinking of visiting my mom soon to get away from all this weird stuff." I thought of driving the Camaro on the freeway. Heavenly. Or maybe I could hook up to Route 66. What a kick that would be. "Hey, who is your grapevine connection? You sure have good info."

"Tsk, tsk. You know better than to ask questions like that. Now, tell me about the crime scene you found. You think it's where Cindy was killed?"

"Positive. There was a pair of panties near a shell casing. And a bit further away, closer to the road, I found where the shooter stood taking potshots at me."

"You're amazing. How did you know to look there?"

I told her about talking to Manny, leaving out the part about coercing the girl into giving me his name. "The driver thought he'd seen something in the woods, but wasn't sure. I decided to take a look on the way home."

"My God, Indie, you need to be more careful. You should've called the sheriff and let them do the searching."

"Yeah, the same way they did the searching for bullet holes in the Bug. It was no big deal. Honestly. I just stopped by the side of the road on the way home." I could tell Ruby was truly worried.

"All the same, stay out of it. There are too many things happening for it to be coincidental and I don't want you to get hurt."

"As it turns out, it's a good thing I *did* stop to look. I went home, found Peter sleeping on the couch and dragged him out there as soon as he woke up. It was only a few hours, but the shell casings had disappeared, at least the ones by the road."

"Oh, Indie, that's terrifying. It means whoever killed Cindy went back, not long after you left the area."

"I'm trying not to think about that."

"Listen, I've got a client call on the other line. I'll talk to you again soon, okay? How about lunch later this week?"

"Sure, see ya later. Let me know if you hear more about Gerry."

I drove to the office with him on my mind. *Why would anyone murder a drunken bass player? How could a town without significant crime suddenly become a hotbed of criminal activity?* A murder rap seemed like high stakes for a few electronics.

The Camaro fit neatly into the last available spot in the courthouse parking lot. Nearly time for the main doors to close, but I dashed into my office to grab a copy of a U.S. Supreme Court brief from my file cabinet. One of our local attorneys frequently hired me to proofread his documents and they usually proved sufficiently fascinating to keep me awake all night working. Good thing because I should have finished this one days ago.

An unnerving quiet held sway over the courthouse as I left my office. Nearly 5 o'clock, but the usual end-of-the-day banter was missing. Okay, maybe the staggered shifts, meaning some people had to work later, played a part in the unusual quiet, but it seemed strange, nonetheless. I peered into the county clerk's office to see some of the deputies turning off their computers and gathering documents. All in complete silence. Weird. Same thing in the treasurer's office.

"Psst, hey." I tried to catch the attention of a young girl putting files into a cabinet. "What's going on?"

"Oh, hi. Sorry, didn't hear you come in." She rubbed her eyes. "You haven't heard? That guy who was killed today, that musician. He was engaged to Rhoda's daughter. Everyone is terribly upset."

Stunned, I wandered out of the office. *How could we not have known he had a fiancé? Did any of the other guys in the band know?* I stopped in the middle of the lobby, troubled by the enormity of the situation. *Gerry had a fiancé, yet he's spent the last few years as an obnoxious drunk. Who would put up with that behavior?*

A small group of women caught my attention just outside the glass front door. Several sat on a bench, while others ranged around them. Bob Williston, the middle-aged county clerk, paced nearby, looking uncomfortable. A young woman, the apparent focus of the group, sobbed softly, her face buried against Rhoda's shoulder.

"Take her home, Rhoda. Don't worry about coming back to work. Stay home the rest of the week, too. She's going to need you." Bob patted the young woman's shoulder awkwardly and dashed into the courthouse.

Rhoda helped the girl to her feet and they left as the well-wishers dispersed to return to their offices.

"Poor thing. She's so distraught."

"…and the wedding only three weeks away."

"I think I'll bake a chicken for them. Nobody feels like cooking when there's a death and they'll need to eat."

I sat on the now vacant bench, watching the comings and goings from the courthouse as my thoughts whirled. A bearded man walked past, tapping his new license plates against the palm of his hand. Judge Oldham and Shawn Trellicki, deep in conversation, walked into the sheriff's office. A huge husky lunged and tugged against his leash, wagging his tail at his owner's entreaties to stop.

A busy place, our courthouse. Kind of fun to sit here for a bit of people watching.

A loud click sounded behind me. Someone had locked the front doors to make the end of the day official. *Time to go home.* I walked to the parking lot and climbed into the Camaro just as an unfamiliar yellow car pulled up in front of the sheriff's office. The passenger leaned over and kissed the driver. I couldn't see clearly through the smoke-tinted windows, but it made me smile. *Wife or girlfriend dropping off a new deputy, I bet.*

The passenger door opened and one booted-foot poked out the door before the person turned his head to glance over at the Camaro. The foot retracted and the door closed.

How sweet-he wanted to give her one last kiss. I drove home with a smile on my face.

Chapter Eleven

"Soon, Mother, soon. I promise." I tried to quell my irritation. After all, I had called *her*, seeking comfort.

"This week? You need some time away from there, Indie. The things I hear from you and Lucille are frightening. There's something strange going on in Oakdale and I'd feel better if you'd get out of there."

"No, not this week, Mother. I promised Ruby I'd watch the kids this weekend so she and Mark can spend the weekend at their cabin."

"Next week then?"

"Maybe. I'll let you know as soon as I decide. I'll talk to you later, okay? I have to proofread this brief. It really should be finished tomorrow and it's a long one."

"Okay, call me tomorrow when you're done with it. Love you, Indie. Your dad says hello."

"Bye, Mom. Love to you both."

I dressed in my coziest flannel pajamas, made a cup of coffee and flopped onto the couch with my red pencil and the brief. By the time I'd finished, the clock read 3 a.m. and I was almost too tired to sleep when I finally crawled into bed.

After a few hours of tossing and turning, dreaming of strange noises and frightening people, my eyes popped open at 7 a.m. I gave up trying to sleep, dragged myself out of bed and into the kitchen to start the coffee pot. My favorite fragrance soon permeated the room and improved my mood as I sat at the table rubbing grit from my burning eyes. Two cups later, I headed for the shower.

I dressed in jeans and a pastel striped shirt, hoping the colors would make me feel more, well, *sprightly. You're a dork, but you know that, right?* I grinned at myself in the mirror, dragging a comb through my wet hair. *Better call Steve today, see if he's heard anything about funeral services for Gerry and I'll let Peter know I'll be at Ruby's all weekend, watching the kids.*

No answer at Peter's number, but Anita answered on the first ring. "Oh, hi, Indie. Terrible news about Gerry, isn't it?"

"Yes, it's unbelievable. Have you heard anything about funeral services?"

"Yes, Friday afternoon at 2. Brady is handling the arrangements and he called Steve this morning to let him know."

"Okay, thanks, Anita. Give the kids a hug and tell Steve I'll see him Friday."

"Will do. Bye, Indie."

I sat the phone on the counter and poured another cup of coffee. *I'll drop the brief off first, then...* My Beethoven ringtone interrupted the mental listing of my day's schedule. "Hello."

"Hi, Indie. It's Ruby."

"Hey, I was going to call you later and let you know Gerry's funeral service is Friday."

"I have court all day Friday and I don't think Judge Oldham will allow a continuance, even for a funeral. He's been quite determined to finish this juvie case. The parents are fighting sending their daughter out of state and the trial has already been rescheduled several times."

"That's okay. You didn't know Gerry that well."

"True, but I would like to be there anyway. I'll file a motion to continue and see what happens. That reminds me—do you know if Cindy's parents set a date for services? I've called several times to express my condolences, but haven't managed to catch them at home. Maybe they aren't answering the phone."

"No, I haven't heard anything, but I have some running around to do today. I'll be glad to stop by and ask."

"Great. Thanks, Indie. I owe you one, but I gotta run. I'll talk to you later, okay?"

"Yep and I'll see you this weekend."

"Oh, wait. I nearly forgot—you're off the hook for babysitting. Amy has the flu, so Mark and I are staying home this weekend."

"Are you sure? I don't mind playing nursemaid."

"Thanks, but no. She gets so upset when she's ill and I know she'll want us both home."

"Okay, but if you change your mind, just holler."

"You're a pal. Thanks, Indie."

I finished my coffee, rinsed the cup and set it on the counter beside the coffee maker. No sense in putting it in the cupboard because I knew I'd use it as soon as I returned home. Ah, coffee…the staff of life. Grinning, I grabbed my purse and the proofed manuscript on the way to the garage, where I spent at least ten minutes admiring the Camaro.

Charley Winslap, the attorney whose legal brief sat on the seat beside me, reigned as a demi-God in his office on the outskirts of town. A tall and ruggedly handsome man with a voice that boomed even when he whispered, Charley kept his office staff scurrying about, endlessly efficient and eager to please. He accepted no excuses, gave no quarter and yet exuded a warm compassion appreciated by friend and foe alike. His ethics were the stuff of legend and his legal documents the epitome of the genre. I adored him in a fatherly, hero-worship kind of way.

"Charley, my man. How goes it?"

"Ah, Indie, my favorite P.I. All goes well here. How's sleuthing?"

I told him about discovering the location of Cindy Brodan's murder.

He shook his head and the great mane of graying hair quivered, but returned to its perfectly groomed position. "Bad business, that whole affair. First, the poor kid lands in juvenile court, and then she winds up in an out of state home for troubled kids. Killed before she makes it home. What were you doing scouting in the woods anyway? What led you to the area?"

"Well, I convinced a girl in the bus terminal…"

Charley laughed and held up a hand. "Wait. Nevermind. I have a feeling the less I know the better. Now, did you finish proof-reading the brief?"

I plopped the thick tome onto his desk. "Yep, here you go. As usual, a superbly written piece. Please never hire anyone else to do your proofreading. It's such a pleasure to read your skillfully crafted documents I'd probably do it for free if I hadn't spent most of my inheritance recently."

"Oh? Pray tell what caught your financial fancy?"

I dragged Charley out to the street where I waxed eloquent on the virtues of the Camaro. After suitable expressions of admiration, he headed back to his office and I jumped behind the wheel to drive out to the Brodan home.

The modest, well-kept house sat on ten wooded acres at the edge of town. A long driveway and a line of poplars at the property edge screened the home from public view. Flowering shrubs shaded several wooden benches beside a small pond, where water gurgled from a center fountain. Near the house, a corral surrounded a tidy barn where several ponies stood saddled and quietly waiting.

I heard the laughter of children as I climbed out of the Camaro and climbed the steps to the front door. After the doorbell rang several times, someone called from the back yard. "We're out back, Helen. Come around."

An astonishing sight greeted me as I rounded the corner of the house.

A world built from a small child's dreams spread across the back acreage. Shrieks of laughter emanated from a huge, bouncy house. Stacks of water toys sat beside an elaborate swimming pool complete with lifeguards. Playground equipment, including an extravagant castle built of stone, covered half an acre. The biggest tree house I've ever seen sprawled between several trees. Adults costumed as cowboys gave lead-line rides on small ponies and a magician performed feats of legerdemain on a well-equipped stage. Half a dozen barbeque grills churned out hot dogs and an immense cotton candy machine spun sugary treats. Dozens of children ran from one entertainment to another, watched over with an indulgent eye by adults sipping fruity drinks.

Not quite the scene of mourning I'd envisioned.

Barty Brodan rose from his lounge chair and sat his drink on a nearby table. With his shoulders back and chin thrust forward, he approached me with narrowed eyes. "This is private property, Miss. I'll have to ask you to leave."

"I'm sorry to intrude. I wanted to extend my condolences at the loss of your daughter."

"It's okay, Barty. Remember Miss Stevens? She worked for that attorney of Cindy's." Marion Brodan extended a slim hand. "Thank you for stopping by, but as you can see, we're entertaining."

"Yes, I see that. Well, Ms. Langston asked me to inquire about the date and time of services for Cindy." I watched as a helium-filled balloon escaped the clutches of its young owner.

Marion and her husband exchanged glances. "You go back to the party, Barty. I'll be there in just a moment."

He nodded at his wife and returned to his lounge chair, turning back once to scowl at me.

Marion touched my shoulder and smiled. "Now, Miss Stevens, we've decided against holding services. Cindy's gone and nothing we can do will change that. Why upset everyone needlessly? It's best just to forget such unfortunate incidents."

"Unfortunate incidents? Mrs. Brodan, you do understand that someone *murdered* your daughter, don't you?" *What the hell kind of twilight zone is this?*

Her eyes instantly hardened, but she maintained her plastic smile. "There's no need to become upset, Miss Stevens. We have our son to think of, you know."

"Yes, well, I shall inform Ms. Langston there will be no service." That beautiful, troubled girl— murdered and discarded beside the highway like a piece of litter while her family threw a party. I thought I might scream if I spent another minute talking to this woman and I couldn't wait to get the hell out of Dodge.

"Mommy, Mommy." The small boy tugged at Marion's pristine skirt and looked at her with a petulant, chocolate-smeared face.

"Yes, dear?" Marion gazed with adoration at her son.

"Mommy, I'm bored. I don't like that boy. He won't play with me." He pointed to a dark-haired boy climbing on the playground equipment.

Eyes glowing with love, she kissed the boy on the forehead. "That's okay, darling. Mommy will help you find something to do. If you'll see yourself to your car, Ms. Stevens…I must attend to my child. Thank you for your concern and good day."

I knew a dismissal when I heard one. Time to escape this nightmare. I glanced around at the adult guests before I trotted around the corner of the house. Distinguished company for a small parts-store owner and part-time librarian. The mayor, Johnny Rucker and his wife, Belinda. Minnie Oldham, the judge's matronly wife. Mr. and Mrs. Browning, both well-known local authors. Others I didn't recognize.

Even the Camaro failed to sooth my soul as I headed back to town.

"Now, calm down, Indie. People deal with grief in different ways. Sorry. There's a storm over here and I'm not getting much of a signal on my cell phone." Ruby's soothing voice cut in and out.

"Yeah, it's kinda hard to hear you. Listen, I know people handle grief in their own way, but I saw no evidence of mourning. I'm telling you there's something wrong. Why else wouldn't there be a funeral service for Cindy?"

"That does seem strange, but still… Maybe their son is having a hard time dealing with his sister's death and they're worried about him."

"That's not the feeling I got. There's something odd going on around here."

"I'm sorry, Indie. You may be right, but it's really none of our business. No law requires these people to mourn the loss of their daughter, no matter how bizarre their behavior seems. I'll call you back later when the storm's over, okay?"

"Yeah, sure. Later."

****

I perched on the edge of the desk and stared out my office window. *Storm must be heading this way.* A heavy layer of dark clouds blanketed the sky. For some reason, the graduated shades of gloom reminded me of accordion keys. One note leading to another. *One murder leading to another.* Trying to shake off my morbid thoughts, I watched the trees bend and twist in the wind like high priestesses dancing before a goddess. *Woops. Your nerd is showing again, Indie.*

The bothersome scene at the Brodans' house refused to leave my mind. *Has the entire world gone mad?* A man murdered in my office for no apparent reason, a man who had no reason to be in my office. A teenage girl murdered, probably by the same person who tried to kill me. The victim's family holds parties, not funeral services. An alcoholic musician murdered, possibly the victim of surprised burglars, who steal nothing but electronics.

No matter how hard I tried, I couldn't see a connection. Working simply wasn't an option in my current state of funk. Suddenly, I longed for the feel of my violin in my hands. *How does that song go...Give me the Beach Boys to free my soul, I wanna get lost in your rock and roll and drift away.* I dug my car keys out of my purse and headed home.

It took some time to tune my poor neglected violin, but eventually I sat at the kitchen table with a steaming cup of coffee in front of me and my beloved instrument in hand. A few measures of *Westphalia Waltz* improved my mood. *Old Joe Clark, Turkey in the Straw* and *Cajun Fiddle* brought a smile to my face and I knew again that music would always revive me. *Maybe it's time for a jam session, even if we don't have a bass player.* I picked up the phone to call Steve, but Anita answered.

"Sorry, Indie, but Steve forgot his cell phone here at the house. I was going to call and ask him to pick up a gallon of milk on his way home. Guess I'll have to do it myself. Who knows how long he and Brady will be at Gerry's place."

"They went to Gerry's?"

"Yes, one of the sheriff's deputies found a will in Gerry's desk. He left everything to Brady. Not much there, but Brady asked Steve to go with him."

"Hm, maybe I'll run out there. I wanted to talk to them about finding a new bass player. You want me to ask him to get milk?"

"Oh, would you? I've got piles of laundry and was hoping to get it caught up."

"Sure, I'll head over there now. If I don't catch Steve at Gerry's, I'll bring it to you myself."

"You don't have to do that, Indie."

"It's no trouble, Anita. Honestly. I can't seem to settle myself to do anything useful today."

"Thanks, Indie. I owe you one unburned dinner."

I'd only been in Gerry's house once. He'd invited everyone to a jam session and barbeque when he'd first bought the place. It was a small, one-bedroom house on the outskirts of town. Living room, kitchen and bathroom downstairs, bedroom and second bathroom upstairs. A previous owner had built an addition on the west side for use as a craft room. Cleared of shelving and furniture, except armless chairs, it served as a perfect place for jamming.

We'd only used it once because Gerry had never invited any of us a second time. He became evasive when asked, so we'd gone back to using my tiny living room. It was better than no practice place, but we all felt crowded and it was a relief when Steve and Anita bought their place with the big shop.

I pulled into Gerry's driveway and climbed out of the Camaro to look around. The place had deteriorated since I'd last seen it. Peeling paint dangled in strips beneath the front windows. The front porch sagged in the middle as if it had given up on life. Someone had kicked aside shards of glass from a broken pane in the front door and trash, mostly empty beer bottles, littered the lawn.

Geez, what a mess. Did the guy bring his fiancé here? I climbed over the broken bottom step to push the doorbell.

"Come on in." Steve's muffled voice called from somewhere inside.

I stepped through the doorway and tried to hold my breath. The overpowering stench made my eyes water and my stomach churn. "God, what's that smell?"

"Rotting garbage, rancid food, filthy dishes. You name it." Steve tried to wipe his watering eyes on the inside of his shirtsleeve without using the latex gloves encasing his hands. "Come on in. Brady's in the kitchen, but I gotta warn ya, the worst of the smell is coming from there."

"Hey, Indie. Long time no see." A gag interrupted Brady's smile. "Sorry. We've only been here half an hour, but it's getting to me."

I sympathized—I'd been here just a few minutes, but my eyes already burned even though every window in the house hung wide open. "Okay, I'm game. Where are the gloves?"

We worked for hours, taking frequent breaks to run outdoors and gulp fresh air. Steve and Brady hauled out bags of trash while I washed dishes. Well, some of the dishes-many had sat so long food and mold had bonded to the surface. Those I tossed into the garbage for the guys to haul to the dumpster.

"I hate to walk out on you, but I've got to get home. Chores for the missus, you know." Steve gave Brady a mock punch. "I'll come back tomorrow if you want."

Brady snapped off his latex gloves. "No problem, mate. I've had enough for one day, too. C'mon, Indie. I'll buy you a cup of coffee."

"You guys go ahead. I want to bleach the countertop so the kitchen is finished. You can buy me a cup of coffee when the entire house is finished." I stepped outside to wave goodbye. "Oh, Steve, Anita wants you to bring home a gallon of milk."

"Why didn't she just call me?" He patted his shirt pocket. "Ah, no phone. So you must have stopped by the house?"

"No, just called to see what you guys thought about setting up a jam session."

"I'll check with Anita and get back to you both, okay?"

Brady and I nodded.

I watched until both cars drove out of sight before climbing over the bottom step again. The house seemed creepy with Steve and Brady gone. A clean breeze blew through the open windows, but the stench refused to dissipate. I poured undiluted bleach on the tile countertops in the kitchen and left it to do its magic while I wandered back to the living room.

The guys had filled four bags with trash from this room before I arrived, but it still needed work. I grabbed the broom and dustpan from the kitchen and started sweeping. Dust motes glittered in the sunlight streaming through the open windows as I emptied the dustpan for the fourth time. *Might as well do this right.* A quick search of Brady's supplies in the kitchen revealed a mop and bucket.

Shoving the furniture to one side of the room, I swept again and then mopped half the room. The floor dried quickly in the breeze and I tugged and shoved the furniture to the side of the room I'd cleaned. Gerry's desk proved heavy and problematic. It was ancient, solid oak and, I swear, weighed as much as the Camaro. I heaved and wrenched, pulled and pushed. Finally, one corner stood far enough out from the wall for me to squeeze behind it and shove. With a loud screech, it swung away from the wall.

Good enough. At least I can clean the trim and leave it for the guys to put back in place. The dust and lint lay so thick the broom did more scraping than sweeping. Bits of broken glass and paper, beer bottle tops, all sorts of trash. A small square of paper stuck to the wall, jammed against the trim. I jabbed at it with the broom, knocking it loose and sweeping it into the dustpan. *One last trip to the trash can to empty this and I'm outta here.*

Suddenly, I couldn't wait to leave. The smell and filth worked on my nerves, making the house seem dark despite the sunshine and fresh air wafting through the open windows and doors. Every creak upstairs sounded like footsteps and each drip of the kitchen faucet like a gunshot.

I forced myself to set the dustpan down and close the windows. *Stop being ridiculous. Just finish this and go home.* With the broom returned to the closet, I tipped the dustpan over the garbage can. Something caught my eye as the paper square fluttered into the garbage can. I grabbed it and tapped the dust and dirt off before turning it over.

It wasn't a square of paper, but a photograph. Using the bottom edge of my t-shirt, I wiped off the dirt obscuring the subject. With horror, I recognized the young girl in the photograph as well as the location.

Cindy Brodan, wearing nothing but a bra and pink panties, stood in the woods on the outskirts of town.

Chapter Twelve

What should I do? Call the police? No, Peter. I can call Peter. Peter's phone rang until his voice mail cut in. I left a message, but I didn't want to wait for his call. I had to get out of here. The overpowering smell, knowing Gerry had died in this room, finding the photograph of Cindy. It was all too much. I shoved the picture into a pocket as I ran out the door, leapt over the broken step and jumped into my car, tearing up the driveway in my hurry to get far, far away from the horrible place.

I left the Camaro in the driveway with the doors locked and fumbled for my front door key. *My God, you're becoming paranoid.* Forcing myself to take a deep breath and slow down, I managed to open the front door. Hearing the deadbolt snap into place made me feel better, safer.

Time to stop acting like a frightened teenager. *You're an investigator, so investigate.* In the kitchen, I made a cup of coffee and let the warmth of the mug in my hands calmed my nerves. I sipped as I pulled the photograph from my pocket and then, used a towel to wipe the last traces of dirt from the surface.

Cindy stood among the trees in dappled sunlight. She didn't look frightened, more puzzled. Her gaze seemed directed somewhere to the photographer's left. *What's that?* I turned on the overhead light to get a better look. No mistake. Two partial shadows revealed the presence of not one, but two people, in addition to the girl.

You're withholding evidence. I knew I had to give the photograph to the police, but the thought of the earlier missing evidence, ala my Volkswagen Bug, bothered me. Taking the photograph to my tiny home office, I made several copies using good quality paper and locked all but one in my file cabinet. I tucked a copy in my purse, the original in my pocket and dashed outside to jump back into the Camaro.

I'll take it to Peter, if he's home. Maybe he doesn't answer his phone because he's sleeping off a night shift. If not, I'll go straight to the sheriff's department, but I'll make them sign for it.

Peter's car sat in front of his apartment, a small yellow car parked beside it. The second car looked familiar, but I couldn't quite place it. That little puzzle solved itself when Peter's door opened and a woman stepped out. Long blond hair, petite, pretty. I froze in the act of opening my car door, watching the scene unfold.

Peter laughed as the woman turned back to say something. Then, he grabbed her arm and pulled her to him. She stood on tiptoes to kiss him before climbing into the yellow car and driving off. He watched her car drive away without spotting me.

Stunned, I sat in the Camaro, collecting my thoughts and sorting my feelings.

A few moments later, the front door opened again and Peter came out dressed in his uniform. He saw me as he unlocked his car door. With hesitant steps and a wary look on his face, he walked over to my window and leaned down. "Hi, Indie. What are you doing here?"

I swallowed the comments that leaped to mind. *Time for that later.* "I need to talk to you, Peter. It's important."

He knew I meant it. "Come on inside. I'll call Shawn to let him know I'll be a little late."

We walked into the kitchen and I pretended not to notice the two coffee cups parked cozily side by side on the table. Nor the two plates stacked beside the omelette skillet in the dish drain. *How sweet. They are playing house.* I gave myself a mental kick. *Knock it off, Indie. It's time for evidence talk, not sarcasm. Give him a chance to tell you on his own terms.*

"Coffee?"

I hadn't noticed him return, but he stood with the pot in one hand, eyebrows raised and dark hair falling across his forehead. *Damn, he's good looking.* "Sure, thanks."

He handed me a yellow mug and sat across from me. "What is it, Indie?"

I pulled the photograph from my pocket and handed it to him.

His sudden inhalation cued me that he'd seen the significance. "Where did you get this?"

"Gerry's house. He left the whole mess to Brady for some reason. I was out there helping Brady and Steve clean the place."

"Have you shown this to anyone else? Told anyone else?"

"No, I brought it straight to you. I tried to call you, but you didn't answer."

The tips of his ears turned red. "Sorry, guess I didn't hear the phone."

I waved a hand, beginning to feel a perverse enjoyment of the situation. "Left the ringer off again?" He mumbled something unintelligible and my conscience made me stop. "No matter. I swept the living room in Gerry's house and emptied the dustpan into the trash. That's when I saw the photo."

"Thanks. I'll take it to work and see it gets to the proper people. I'd appreciate it if you don't mention this to anyone."

"No problem, except you know I will tell Ruby."

He considered this for a moment. "I wish you wouldn't, but I suppose it's alright. Cindy was Ruby's client. Ask her to keep it to herself though."

I nodded and sipped from my mug.

"I don't want to rush you, but I need to get to work. You're welcome to stay to finish your coffee."

"Thanks, but I need to get moving, too. Lots to do." I tipped the dregs from the cup and placed it beside the two plates.

He trailed behind me as I walked out the door. "See you, Indie."

Uh-oh. Awkward moment. I knew he was thinking of our usual goodbye kisses, but I wanted to forestall any pretense, even if he didn't know I'd seen the other woman. Faking a cheery wave, I climbed into the Camaro and drove home.

I'd enjoyed the freedom and privacy of living alone since moving out of my parents' home, but the house seemed empty today. Feeling lost, I dialed Ruby's number and wandered into the kitchen for a cup of coffee.

"What's wrong? You sound funny."

"Nothing, nothing. Well, it's Peter." I meant to tell her about the photograph, but found myself spilling my guts about seeing the woman coming out of Peter's apartment.

"That rat. How could he do such a thing? I have a hearing with Judge Oldham tomorrow. I'll come over early and have a talk with Peter." Ruby fumed.

"No, don't bother." A thought struck me. "I didn't tell him. Besides, I think it may be for the best."

"What does that mean?"

"I'm not sure. Not really." I'd remembered where I'd seen the yellow car. Outside the sheriff's department, dropping someone off. "Listen, I actually called to tell you about something else. I found a photograph of Cindy, maybe taken at the same place where she was killed."

"What? Where did you find it? You're not nosing around in some place where you'll get into trouble, are you?"

"Slow down." She sounded frantic, but at least I'd distracted her from the subject of Peter. "No, I found it in Gerry's house."

"Gerry's house? That's crazy. Why would he have a picture of Cindy?"

"I don't know. Not yet."

"I want to see it. I'd like to find out what happened to her. What makes you think somebody took it right before she was killed?"

"Ruby, I'd rather show it to you than talk about it. I have a few things to do today, so stop by tomorrow and I'll make you a latte, okay?"

"Sure. I'll be over after my hearing."

As soon as she hung up, I called Steve. "If you and Brady aren't busy, would you meet me at Gerry's house? I need your help."

"Thank God. Anita's been after me to take her shopping for drapes and this is a great escape for me."

"Tell her I'll take her this weekend if she can wait."

"Okay. Hang on a minute." Steve covered the phone and I heard muffled voices. "All set. She said she'd rather go with you anyway. Says you have better taste."

Anita laughed and I grinned. "I hear her. Okay, how soon can you be there?"

"I'll call Brady and be right there. There's a key under the doormat if you get there first."

The house sat silent and dark when I pulled into the driveway and the hair on my arms rose before I stepped out of the car. Bare tree branches stretched upward in supplication to the harvest moon, rattling in the breeze. An owl hooted in the distance and a faint tang of woodsmoke hung in the air.

Your imagination is working overtime, girlfriend. Just get the key and turn on the lights. After several minutes of fumbling with the doormat, I found the key, slipped inside and then ran through the house like a maniac turning on lights. When I had Brady's electric bill burning up his paycheck, I felt sufficiently calm to sit at the kitchen table planning my next move.

Not in here. We've cleaned it from inside out. Ditto on the living room. The bedroom? Something about the idea of searching the bedroom made me shudder. *No, I'll wait for Steve and Brady. Let them do that one. That leaves only the basement.*

I dug around in the kitchen drawers until I found a flashlight. The dim beam didn't illuminate much when I tested it, but I felt safer knowing I had a backup. You know, in case the power went off or something. Who wants to be in a strange basement in the dark?

The front door burst open. Just as I crossed the kitchen and rounded the corner to the basement stairs. "Is that you Steve? Brady?"

Nobody answered, but heavy footsteps thudded my way. I shrank against the wall with no place to run or hide. With every light in the house blazing, whoever stomped through the house toward the hall couldn't miss seeing me. My heart pounded and the flashlight slipped from my damp palms to land on the floor with a loud bang.

The overhead light glinted off a gun aimed straight at my heart.

Chapter Thirteen

"Shawn." I leaned weakly against the wall and exhaled. Shawn Trellicki, Peter's partner, stopped at the end of the hall holding his gun with an unwavering grip and staring at me through narrowed eyes. "Thank God, it's you. You scared me half to death."

Without lowering the gun, he took a step forward. "What are you doing here?"

"Sheesh, put the gun away, will you? It's freaking me out."

"Hey, what's going on here? What happened to the door? Indie, where are you?" Brady sounded aggravated. "Damn, the lock is broken."

Shawn continued to stare, dropping the gun and tucking it into his holster only as the guys rushed into the hall. He turned with an easy smile. "Brady, Steve. I happened to drive by and saw all the lights. Thought maybe you had a burglar or somebody messing with the crime scene."

Brady's forehead wrinkled and his sweet, pudgy face crinkled in a frown. "Crime scene? The sheriff's department released the house days ago."

"Yes, well, you never know. People like to gawk at the scene of a murder. Figured I'd better check it out."

Still a bit shaky over the idea of a gun pointed at me, I dredged up a skiff of dignity and a smidgeon of righteous anger.

"Hey, what about Brady's door? You had no right or reason to kick in the door."

Shawn shot a venomous look at me. "Yeah, sorry about the door. I'll talk to the department about it. If they won't cover it, I'll pay for it myself."

Brady scratched his chin. "Okay I guess, but next time, knock first."

"Yeah. See you guys later." Shawn swaggered to the front door, pausing to cast another cold look at me before he left.

"What the hell was that about? That guy's got a problem." Brady bent to inspect the splintered doorframe as Steve tucked my arm under his and steered me to the couch.

"Geez, you're shaking. I guess having somebody kick the door in would scare me, too." Steve handed me his own travel mug filled with coffee.

A bit too sweet for me, but not bad. "Thanks, Steve. I'm glad you guys got here when you did."

"I'll get somebody out here to fix this tomorrow. Don't have time to do it myself." Brady shook his head. "I sure wish Gerry had left this place to someone else."

"So if you're recovered from your scare, tell us what's going on. Why did you ask us to meet you?" Steve plopped himself on the other end of the couch.

"Did either of you notice the gun?" I watched their faces as surprise registered.

"Gun?" Brady snagged a chair and pulled it closer.

"Trellicki pulled his gun and pointed it at me."

Steve's eyes widened. "Wow, must have scared you to death, but you probably startled him, too."

"No, he…" I knew if I told them Shawn had questioned me while pointing the gun at my heart, I would sound hysterical. "You're probably right."

"If you're ready to move on, why did you ask us here? I don't want to rush you, but I promised Anita I'd be home to help her get the kids to bed." Steve yawned.

Brady laughed. "Huh, I don't think so. I think you want to go to bed yourself."

"Maybe so. It's been a long day."

"Okay, here's the scoop." I explained I had found a photograph earlier while sweeping. "I thought you two could help me search the rest of the house. I figure three sets of eyes are better than one. Besides, it's Brady's house now."

"Don't be silly. You know you're welcome anytime, Indie." Brady paused. "But, what are we looking for?"

"I'm not sure. Anything out of place, things that shouldn't be here. Something that strikes you as wrong."

They both looked doubtful, but Steve volunteered to search the garage and Brady the bedroom. That left only the basement.

I stood at the top of the stairs, shaking off a sense of unease. Flipping the light switch, I stomped down the steps.

The basement proved surprisingly clean and tidy. Freshly painted white walls, recently swept floor. A furnace stood in one corner. Shelves covered all four walls. Nothing down here except a few old canning jars and a stack of empty, dusty cardboard boxes.

"Indie? I think you'd better come up here."

I could see Brady in the doorway above me. He clutched a small box, holding it away from his body and eyeing it warily.

"Here, you take this. I don't know if it's what you're looking for, but I know I want nothing to do with it. What the hell was wrong with Gerry?"

I took the box and carried it to the living room while Brady, looking as if he'd eaten something that disagreed with him, marched ahead of me. The box felt odd and somehow wrong. Evil. Shaking my head at my own folly, I sat the box on the couch and lifted the lid.

My first sight of the contents made me nauseous and faint. The box held photographs. Horrible, terrible, evil photographs. Depictions of children in various states of undress, child pornography. I slammed the lid down and rushed outside the shattered front door, breathing deeply of the cool night air.

Brady followed me through the door and put a gentle arm around my shoulders. "Are you okay, Indie? It was a real shock when I opened that box. I think we should take it to the police."

"Nothing in the garage. Hey, what's going on? You sick, Indie?" Steve bounded over the broken step to join us on the porch.

"Open the box sitting on the couch." Brady jerked a thumb toward the front door.

Steve returned in a few seconds, his face pale in the moonlight. "Where the hell did those come from? That's sick, man."

"I found the box on a shelf in the bedroom closet. Must have been Gerry's." Brady turned to stare at the house. Light spilled onto the front porch through the shattered front door, illuminating the broken step and peeling paint. "I have no idea why Gerry decided to leave this place to me, but I wish he hadn't. It was bad enough before but, the place gives me the creeps now."

"I'll help you board up the broken door, but let's get out of here after, okay? No offense, Brady, but I think you should sell it as is. No more cleaning." Steve shivered.

"No offense taken. I feel the same way. Indie, what do you think we should do with that box?"

"We need to give it to the authorities." A heavy weight settled on my chest, leaving me short of breath. I knew they would ask me to handle it, but the thought of having possession of the box and its contents made me nauseous. *C'mon, give 'em a break. They have to fix the door and they're spooked. You're supposed to be the investigator, the one who works in the legal system. Buck up.* "I'll take the box to Peter, if you like, but you carry it to the car." *At least I won't have to touch the damned thing again.*

The guys wedged the box into the trunk so the photos wouldn't dump out and then made me promise to call when I reached town.

"If we don't hear from you in half an hour, we'll come looking. No more wandering around alone in the dark like the night of the storm. Thanks, Indie." Brady squeezed my shoulder.

"Are you sure you don't want one of us to ride with you?"

"No, I'll be fine. I promise to go straight to Peter's apartment."

"Okay, but lock your car doors and I mean it. Keep them locked until you get to Peter's." Steve shook a finger when I grinned at him.

The drive to Peter's apartment proved uneventful, although I spooked myself by jumping at every shadow on the road. No lights on in his place. No car in front. I called Steve to let him know I'd arrived and then, I dialed Peter's cell phone.

He answered on the first ring. "Hello, Indie."

"Are you busy? I have something for you." I heard voices and laughter in the background. Tinkle of glasses, the clink of silverware. Sounds like—*a dinner date with the mysterious woman?*

"Uh, is it important? I'm kind of busy right now."

I stifled a flare of annoyance and... *Jealousy? Maybe.* "I hate to interrupt you, but yes, it's important."

He grunted. "Hmph, fine, where are you?"

"Parked in front of your apartment." I heard muffled voices; one sounded vaguely female and argumentative. Yeah, I admit feeling a tiny mote of satisfaction. *Take that, biatch.* Okay, maybe more than a mote.

"Give me twenty minutes."

"I'll be here." Reading the news and playing games on my phone entertained me for a short time, but I soon found myself lacking interest. I shut off the phone and tucked it into my pocket.

The streetlight on the corner cast a feeble glow, illuminating only a small area at its base. Feeling cocooned by the pressing darkness, I rolled down my window in time to hear two drunks arguing as they entered the apartment two doors down from Peter's. A teenager rode past on a bicycle. A quiet street in our quiet town.

Quiet on the surface, but not so peaceful anymore. I shivered thinking about the box in my trunk. Why did Gerry have those photos? I couldn't believe he had any interest in child pornography, but how well did I really know him? Before his wife left him, he seemed a pleasant guy. A terrific bass player, friendly, generous. Honest, or so I used to think.

I picked up my cell phone to check the time as loud rap on my window startled me and I jumped, banging my head on the roof of the car.

"Indie? You awake?" Peter stood beside my car.

I hadn't noticed him parking across the street. *Some observant PI.*

"Come on inside." His keys jingled as he took them from his pocket, the sound echoing around the small cul d sac.

"Just a minute. There's a box in my trunk. Would you mind carrying it inside for me?"

"A box?" He stood close enough for me to smell his musky aftershave.

"Evidence." I watched him lean over the back of the car and take out the box. Even by the dim light of the trunk, he looked gorgeous in his suit and tie. *Hey, he never took me any place grand enough to wear a suit and tie.*

"Evidence? What kind of evidence?"

"Wait until we're inside, okay? Steve, Brady and I found this in Gerry's house." I followed him into the kitchen where he set the box on the table before he removed his jacket and tie.

He reached for the box.

"Hang on. Would you open it somewhere else?" I hesitated. "I know it sounds childish, but I feel sick knowing I'm even near it."

He stared at me for a moment with those meltingly beautiful eyes before taking the box into the living room. I paced around the kitchen, finally settling to make a pot of coffee. Halfway through my second cup, Peter returned.

He peeled off a pair of rubber gloves and tossed them into the trash. "Did anyone else touch the photos?"

"I didn't, but you'll have to ask Brady and Steve." I shuddered.

"How did you find the box?"

"I didn't. Brady found it." I closed my eyes and sipped from my mug. *Decent, but not his usual dark roast. His new girlfriend must have chosen this.*

"What was Brady doing in Gerry's house?"

"Gerry willed the house to Brady. Steve and I helped him clean the place so he can sell it. I found the photo of Cindy stuck to a wall behind Gerry's desk. Brady found the box in the bedroom closet."

He gave me a sharp glance. "You need to stay out of this one, Indie. I don't know if Cindy's death is connected to that box of photos, but I think it's going to turn dangerous."

"There's something else." I hesitated, knowing how close law enforcement partners become when they work together.

"This isn't a good time to be reticent." He leaned back in his chair.

"You're right, but you aren't going to like this." I told him about Shawn pointing his gun at me and not lowering it until Steve and Brady's fortuitous arrival. His lack of surprise disturbed me. "Aren't you going to say something? How about 'gee, Indie, that's scary. I'll check into it.' Or even, 'you're crazy, woman,' would be better than nothing."

"I'm sorry. It's been a long day and I'm too tired to think. You know I take these things seriously."

My heart rate increased and I couldn't quell the sudden wave of anger that washed over me. "Maybe if you weren't so busy taking another woman out to dinner and sleeping with her, you wouldn't be so tired." If I'd expected anger or shame, I was disappointed.

He slumped in the chair with a pale face and shadowed eyes. "How long have you known?"

"Long enough."

He sat up straight and rubbed his eyes. "Listen, I'm sorry. I really am. I wanted to talk to you, but the timing never worked."

"How convenient. You've had time to sleep with someone, but not enough time to tell me? You are sleeping with someone else, but still trying to control everything I do."

"What are you talking about? Control what you do?"

"Yes, I mean that little fit you threw when I told you I'd bought the Camaro. If you were planning to dump me, why would you care about the car?"

His eyes widened. "Dump you? What makes you think that?"

"For God's sake, Peter, you're sleeping with someone else."

"I guess I thought you might change your mind about getting married if you thought you might lose me to someone else."

Yeah, more like you couldn't bear to lose control of one woman before you gained power over another. All of a sudden, I felt deflated and ashamed, not angry. Peter was a nice guy. Just not the one for me. I'd known it for a long time. "Maybe this is as much my fault as yours."

"I'm not sure what you mean."

"You want marriage and family. I don't. At least I don't want them now."

"I guess that's part of it anyway, but I didn't mean for this to happen. I always thought someday we'd marry if I waited long enough."

"That's something I can't promise."

"And I didn't want to press you into marriage if you weren't ready. I'm sorry, Indie. You know I love you." His eyes filled with tears.

"Yes, I know. Let's be adult about this, okay? There's no reason we can't be friends. I wish you only the best with, uh, your new girlfriend." I didn't even know her name, but my gut reaction was relief.

"I think you'd like her. Her name is Terry and she works as a secretary in the juvenile court in the next county." He seemed eager to smooth things over; he probably expected a melodramatic scene.

"I'm sure she's a very nice person. Time for me to head home. It's the middle of the night and it's been a long day." I'm not a drama fan, but the touchy-feely "let's all be friends" was too much for me.

"You're welcome to sleep on the couch. It's late for you to be driving alone."

I knew he was thinking of my disastrous trip home from Steve's house during the storm. "No, I'll be fine. Will you let me know if you find out anything about the photographs?"

A guarded look replaced his over-eager friendliness. "I'll see they get to the right people."

"Yeah, okay. See ya." I grabbed my purse and phone.

He walked me to my car and waited while I fastened my seatbelt. "Indie, I truly am sorry, you know."

"I know." I peeked once in the rear view mirror and saw him staring after me before I turned the corner and he was gone.

Music from the radio and the purr of the Yenko soothed my doubts during the drive home, so that I felt calm and relaxed when I turned onto the street where I lived.

At least until I saw what awaited me.

Chapter Fourteen

The flashing lights of a dozen police cars illuminated the crowd and fire trucks in front of my house. Smoke billowed from the back of the house, although I saw no flames. Several neighbors rushed across the street as I climbed out of the Camaro. Everyone spoke at once and I couldn't make sense of any of it.

The fire chief made a futile attempt at wiping ash and sweat from his face as he gently pushed his way through the crowd. "Excuse me. Move aside, ma'am. Let me through. Are you Miss Stevens, the owner?"

I nodded without speaking. My home, my hard-earned possessions. Gone. Furniture, clothes, laptop, books, violin. *My coffee pot. More than anything else, I could use a cup of coffee right now.* It was too much for one day. First my boyfriend and now my home.

"Are you okay, ma'am?" The fire chief's solicitude did credit to his department.

I wiped the tears from my cheeks and stood straight. After all, I was alive and not in the house when it happened. "What happened?"

"We're not sure yet, but there's a strong smell of gasoline in one of the back rooms."

"Gasoline? Do you mean arson?" *How could that be? Why would someone burn my house?*

He gave my shoulder a fatherly pat. "I know this must be a shock to you, ma'am, but if you'll come with me, I have a few questions."

He led me through the crowd to the rear of the house. "It isn't as bad as it might've been. One of your neighbors spotted the flames and called in the fire. There's some minor smoke damage throughout the house, but only one room is destroyed."

The fire had scorched my office/study like a steak burned to a crisp. Acrid smoke hung in the air making me gag as I peered through the broken window. Blackened walls surrounded the shapeless, charred lumps littering the floor. The door hung drunkenly from its bottom hinge.

"This window was broken when we arrived." The chief stuck out a hand. "Name's Ron, by the way. Ron Beezly. You're Alice's daughter, aren't you? Fine woman, your mother. Now, Ms. Stevens, did you store anything of value in the room? Something somebody might have wanted to steal?"

I shook my head. "No, nothing. This was just my home office. I didn't even keep work files here. Just my desk, a few books. Things like that."

"Okay, well, it sure looks like someone tore the place apart. We'll leave someone here all night until we can get the place boarded up tomorrow. The fire marshal will be here in the morning to conduct his investigation into the cause of the fire. Until then I'm afraid I can't let you inside. Do you have a place you can stay?"

"Yes, but I think I'll check into a motel. It will be closer in case you need me for anything." We exchanged cell phone numbers and I threaded my way through the dwindling crowd to the Camaro.

****

Ellen McKenzie, the motel owner, an old friend of my parents', handed me a room key as well as a new toothbrush, toothpaste, shampoo and a bathrobe. "Here, on the house, you poor thing. Have you told your mother yet?"

"No, I'll call her in the morning. No sense in waking her in the middle of the night. Thanks, Ellen." I bundled up the toiletries and trudged to my room, heading straight to the shower to wash the smell of smoke from my hair.

Just before I drifted off to sleep, I had a thought.

If I hadn't taken the box of photos straight to Peter, they'd have been in my now-ruined office.

****

The fire marshal snapped his notebook closed. "That's it, ma'am. We'll let you know when we get the results back from the lab, but my guess is arson. Thanks for meeting me so early, ma'am. I have another one to go to out on the old highway. It's going to be a long day."

"*Another* arson?" I knew my disbelief rang in my voice.

"Won't know that until I take a look around. Now if you'll excuse me—"

"Wait. Is the address by any chance 454 Highway 2339?"

153

The fire marshal gave me a calculating look, his hand poised in the act of poking his pen into his uniform pocket. "Yes, it is. Do you know something?"

The air whooshed out of my lungs and my heart pounded. I rubbed my clammy palms on my jeans. "It's just that, well, I had a friend who died in his house out there. Another friend inherited the place and we found, well, some photographs."

His eyes narrowed and he re-opened his notebook. "Photographs? You're not making sense, ma'am. Maybe I'd better ask a few more questions."

"Listen, I have to go. I'm visiting my mother for a week or two. Give my insurance company time to have my house cleaned and repaired." *My God, I have to get out of town. I need time to think. Besides, I want to get a look at the school Cindy attended.*

He eyed me with a calculating look.

"Call Deputy Peter Hampton. He can give you the answers you need and he'll know how to contact me at all times." I gave him Peter's cell phone number.

"I may want to talk to you again. Make sure you keep us informed of your phone number." He gave me a look that suggested I might be a crazy arsonist seeking a new target.

"The chief has my contact info. He also knows my family and how to contact them."

He nodded doubtfully and I left.

After stopping to purchase a few necessary items like underwear, I called the insurance company to let them know I'd be out of town. The agent assured me their contractor would complete the repairs before my return.

A cup of coffee from the convenience store and I was ready to hit the road.

After a day's worth of coffee from convenience stores, I was ready to get off the road.

The motel looked nearly deserted with its flickering neon sign and one lonely car in the parking lot, but it was right beside the highway. An old man puttered about the office, watering plants and humming an obscure show tune. "Hello, miss. Can I help you?"

"Yes, I'd like a room for the night."

"Certainly." He took my credit card information and handed over a key. "You're in room eight, two doors to your right. Now, if you're hungry, the local restaurant will deliver to the room for five bucks."

I carried my bag to my room and called to have a small pizza delivered.

"Sorry, ma'am. Our delivery boy is home sick tonight."

One of those days. First your house burns and then, you can't even get a lousy pizza delivered for dinner. I pulled out the clips holding my hair and tossed them on the bedside table. *At least there's coffee.*

The tiny coffee pot filled the room with a mouth-watering aroma while I dressed in my new pajamas. Beethoven sounded as I leaned against a stack of pillows against the bed's headboard.

"Indie, where are you? I've been trying to reach you all day." Ruby sounded panicked.

Damn, I'd forgotten to call her before I left town. "In a little motel on the way to visit my parents. Sorry, I meant to call you before I left, but guess I forgot in all the excitement."

"Excitement is right. Peter called me trying to find you. He said the fire marshal called him asking him to verify that you were with him before the fire."

"Sorry." I truly was sorry. Ruby is a worrier and I should have realized she would panic hearing news of the fire.

"Why didn't you answer your phone? I'm not the only one trying to find you." She blew her nose and I guessed she'd been crying.

Wow, she really freaked out. "The ringer must have been off. Ruby, is something else wrong? I mean, sure, my house burned, but the damage isn't that bad and you knew I was okay if you talked to Peter. Surely the fire chief told him I was fine."

She sniffed and blew her nose again. "Well, I didn't want to tell you. I figured you had enough to worry about with your house."

"What is it? Are the kids okay? Mark?"

"Yes, yes. Everyone is fine. It's just that…" Her voice rose. "Two more children have disappeared."

"What? Who? What the *hell* is going on?"

"I don't know what's going on, but it's terrifying. It's as if all the children in the county have become targets for some crazed psycho. We've put cots in our bedroom for Amy and Tommy. I'm afraid to let them sleep in their own rooms."

"Okay, take a deep breath. Put me on speakerphone and make yourself a cup of coffee." I heard water running and the coffee pot gurgle as we chatted about inconsequentials.

I heard a clunk as she sat a heavy mug on her table. "Now, sit down at the table and tell me what happened."

In a halting voice, she told me someone abducted a child from the grocery store where she shopped and a second child disappeared only two blocks from the courthouse.

"Oh, no. Not again. The whole world has gone insane. What do the police say? Do they have any leads?" I shivered at the thought of the evil creeping over our town.

"I talked to Peter, but he didn't really say much. I think some of the families are demanding that Muley call in the feds."

"He should. This is getting out of hand, like some monstrous pandemic spreading out of control."

"Indie, I have to go. Amy is calling me."

"Of course. I'll talk to you later. Say, is the school taking precautions? With all those kids outside for recess, I'd worry."

"Yes, the school has cancelled all outdoor activities until this person is caught. Mark took vacation time, so he's home with Amy all day and he drives Tommy to and from school. No babysitters."

"Good. That makes me feel better."

"Indie, your house...I'll call you again soon, okay?"

"Call anytime, but don't worry about the house. It'll be fine."

I put my glasses on the bedside table, turned off the light and fell asleep trying to remember how many children had disappeared.

Chapter Fifteen

I arrived at my parents' home late the next evening. Dad snored quietly in his recliner next to the fireplace while Mom helped carry in my two small bags. "Your father was awake reading all night last night. You know how he is. Now, come into the kitchen, dear. I have dinner waiting."

Mom carried a golden-brown chicken pie to the table as Dad wandered into the kitchen, yawning. He gave me a big hug. "I'm so glad you're here. Sorry I fell asleep."

"Hi, Dad. Hey, it's no wonder you fell asleep. It's the middle of the night. It's good to see you both. It's been too long since I visited."

"I've been trying to tell you that for quite some time." Mom deftly lifted a thick slice of pie onto my plate.

"I know. I know. I do have to work to pay the bills, Mom. Besides, you and Dad could visit me, you know." Chunks of chicken and vegetables peeped from beneath a flaky crust and the aroma made my mouth water. *I should be living closer to this bounty. Much better than a bowl of microwaved ramen noodles.* Grinning to myself, I reached for the salad bowl.

After dinner, Dad insisted on carrying my bags upstairs to the guest room. "Now, quit fussing. I may be an old man, but I can still do something for my little girl. Here you go."

"Aw, you're not an old man, Dad and you know it."

He grinned. "Old or not, it's time I went to bed. See you in the morning, Indie. I'm glad you're home."

Mom poked her head through the doorway. "Are you coming to bed? Goodnight, Indie dear."

After they left, I looked around in awe. Everything about the room bespoke calm and comfort, from the pale blue and white walls to the thick carpet underfoot. Overflowing bookcases lined the wall opposite an antique iron bed and the walk-in closet offered ample space for several lifetimes of clothing. A small white desk sat beneath a large window, which provided a panoramic view of Mom's rose garden and the twinkling city lights beyond it. Even the attached pristine bathroom offered hedonistic luxury, such as a glass-walled shower and heated towel rack.

Too weary to explore even the wonders of the bookcase, I struggled into pajamas and crawled beneath the soft lavender-scented bed covers. As I reached to flip off the bedside lamp, I had a sudden vision of my mother tapping her chin with a finger and saying, "Hm, I wonder what might convince Indie to stay."

I fell asleep with a smile on my face.

****

After five days of shopping trips, lazing in a hammock with a book, and gorging myself on my mother's wonderful cooking, I'd gained three pounds and an urge to do something useful. "Mom, I'm heading out. I'll be back in a few hours. You need anything from the store?"

"No thanks, dear. The farmer's market is open tomorrow and I usually get produce there. Where are you going?"

"I promised Ruby I'd pay a visit to a school over on B Street. That's where our juvenile court system sends some of the kids."

"B Street? Now you be careful. That's not a good part of town. Lots of crime and vacant buildings."

"It can't be that bad, Mom. After all, there's a school."

"Hm, I don't remember a school on B Street, but I could be wrong. I don't spend much time in that part of town." Her forehead creased and she shook her head.

"Don't worry, Mom. I promise to be careful and I'll be home soon."

The traffic proved maddening. *No surprise she seldom visits this side of town. How can anyone stand this?* Despite the season, heat waves roiled upward from the huge expanses of road and nearby pavement, creating a watery mirage. Horns honked as impatient drivers urged their fellow drivers to action. A small scooter wove between cars stalled in unmoving lanes, provoking shouts and rude gestures. Cars crept forward a few feet only to halt when the distant traffic light again turned red.

After what seemed like hours and nearly was, I parked the Camaro across from 343 B Street. A couple of vacant warehouses, a store with boarded-up windows, the shabbiest office building I'd ever seen. Nothing on the block resembled a school. Wondering if

I'd copied the address incorrectly, I climbed out of the Camaro and crossed the street.

The ancient door creaked open onto a long hallway dimly lit by one bare bulb dangling from a wire overhead. Tiny clouds of dust poofed into the air with each step on the mouldering carpet, which had lost its color long ago. Rickety doors punctuated walls scarred with graffiti and peeling paint. The odor...arghhh! Old fried fish and litter boxes. *How can anyone breathe in here? Definitely miscopied the address. Damn. All that driving for nothing. Well, maybe somebody here can give me a correct address.*

I paused, trying to stifle my gag reflex at the smell, when I heard voices from an open doorway. Eavesdropping is unethical, so I wasn't indulging. Honest. Is it my fault people leave their office door open and I overhear their conversation?

"Could you repeat that name, sir? Yes, she just stepped into the office. One moment, please." An unseen woman spoke and a beep sounded; someone had put a caller on hold. "Okay, Darcy, you're up. Number thirty-seven, Mrs. O'Reilly."

"Damn and me with my nails still wet." A second female voice grumbled and the phone clicked. "This is Mrs. O'Reilly. May I help you?"

"Lynn, number six, Glenda Billings, on line 3."

"Okay, thank you, Ms. Onco."

Glenda Billings? She was Cindy's teacher. What is this place? Shedding all cautionary instincts, I stepped boldly through the open door. No one noticed me for a few minutes, so I had plenty of time to look around. Nothing made sense.

The dinghy, windowless room held a row of padded cubicles, each furnished with a small desk, folding chair and a telephone. A sharp-eyed woman, dressed in a plain black skirt and long-sleeved white blouse, occupied a desk placed for viewing the cubicle occupants.

"Hello, this is Glenda Billings. May I help you?" A slender woman flicked her blond ponytail and leaned to peer at a list beside her telephone. "Yes, Mrs. Thomas, she's doing quite well. No, she's in class right now, but I'd be happy to send you her latest grade report. I'm sorry, but I must rush off. I have a class to teach right now. Yes, I'll see the report goes out in today's mail. You're very welcome."

"Very nice, Lynn. Remember to log the caller's name as well as the number on the caller ID." Ms. Onco, who apparently used her sharp eyes only to keep her employees in line, finally noticed me. She leaped from her chair and rushed across the dinghy, stained carpet. Her graying hair, pinned in a firm bun, remained resolutely in place as she stormed across the carpet on sturdy, sensible shoes, raising a puff of dust with every stomp. "Who are you? This is a private business. The public is not allowed in this office."

"Excuse me. I didn't mean to intrude, but I'm looking for a school at this address." I held out my hand and smiled.

Ms. Onco ignored the proffered hand and pointed at the door. "You must be mistaken. There is no school here. Now please leave."

Several women turned to watch the exchange, but no one spoke.

I whipped a small notebook from my pocket, flipped it open and pretended to consult written directions. "Is this 343 B Street? Your name is Ms. Onco?"

"I've asked you to leave. Please do so or I shall be forced to call the police."

"The police? Isn't that a rather dramatic response to a request for directions?"

The telephone rang and Ms. Onco cast a desperate glance toward her desk. "Leave. Now. Lynn, please close the door behind our uninvited guest."

As my father says, discretion is the better part of valor. I gave the watching women a smile and a wave as I left. Lynn closed the door quietly behind me, but not before I heard Ms. Onco answer the ringing telephone. "Onagitchee Children's Home. May I help you?"

I tiptoed down the hall, trying to avoid resurrecting the dust cloud. Impossible. No matter how gently I placed my feet, the carpet released a portion of its burden of filth and decay with every step. By the time I reached the door, my formerly white tennis shoes had obtained the same colorless shade as the carpet.

Tapping my feet against the curb, I managed to knock loose some of the dirt from my shoes before taking a couple of shots of the building with my cell phone camera and climbing into the Camaro. As I sat trying to get my bearings for the drive back to my parents' home, the woman with the blond ponytail exited the building. She walked to the end of the block and disappeared into a coffee shop.

I grabbed my purse and jumped from the Camaro to follow her. She sat near a window, chatting with a waitress. I ordered a cup of coffee at the counter and then, crossed the room. "Hi. Mind if I sit down?"

At close range, she appeared older than I'd first thought. Early forties, maybe. Faint lines and wrinkles around the eyes. A bit of gray at the temples. She narrowed her eyes to look at me, but shrugged. "Sure. It's a free country. You're the one who came into the office, aren't you?"

I nodded. "Yes. I promised to look in on a friend's daughter. The kid is attending a school somewhere around here, but I must have the wrong address. You worked there long?"

"About six months. It's boring, but it's a job. I'm an actress and you know struggling actresses have to support themselves somehow. Before you ask, yes, I know most aspiring actresses live in California, but I work in smaller productions. Commercials for local television stations, plays, that sort of thing." She thanked the waitress who brought her salad.

"I'm Indie Stevens." I sipped from my coffee cup. Not bad.

"Indie? That's an unusual name."

"Well, as an actress, you might appreciate this. I don't tell many people, but my real name is Indianetta. My mother named me after a famous character in a movie, although she had to alter the name to suit a girl."

She laughed and visibly relaxed. "I quite like that. I'm Lynn Scoffetto. Are you from around here?"

"No, just visiting my parents. So, is that office some sort of call center? Selling advertising or conducting surveys?"

"No, nothing like that. We answer phones and play different characters. When someone calls the office, Ms. Onco transfers the call to whichever of us plays the role of the person called. We each have a list of names with a paragraph or two of information about the person." She smiled and attacked her salad. "Sorry. I'm starving. Typical actress, always watching my weight, you know."

"Wow, it sounds fascinating. How does a person get a job like that?" I struggled to hide my dismay.

"Most of us got the job through a casting agency, Brentam's Casting. It's not fascinating, though. It's a bit strange. I've never figured out what's going on, but I guess nobody pays me to know. The pay's not bad, but I'm hoping I won't be there much longer. I have an audition tomorrow for a big television commercial. It might be the break I need." She pushed her salad bowl to the side of the table and glanced at her watch. "Eek, I've got to run. An appointment with my personal trainer."

"Let's exchange addresses. If I hear of any job openings for actresses, I'll give you a call." With names and addresses entered into our cell phones, we said goodbye and she rushed off. I sat at the table drinking a second cup of coffee and watching the front door of 343 B Street, wishing for something to happen that would make sense of it all. After half an hour, I gave up and drove back to my parents' house.

****

I opened the Camaro's trunk and tossed in my bags. How did my one small bag become an entire trunkful of parcels? Oh, yeah, shopping trips with Mom. I grinned and walked back to the front step. "Here, I'll take that, Mom."

She held out a travel cup full of to-die-for coffee. "Now, Indie, you call me tonight. I want to know where you are."

"Of course, Mom. Thanks for everything. You, too, Dad. I'll miss you." I hugged them both.

"I don't see why you're in such a hurry to go back."

My heart ached at the look of hurt on Dad's face. "Time for me to get back to work, but I promise I won't wait so long to visit the next time."

The Camaro roared to life and I drove away, glancing in the rearview mirror. They stood together on the front step, Dad's arm around Mom's waist, watching and waving.

Like I told my parents, time to get back to work. My cell phone lay on the passenger seat, holding what I hoped would prove the key to solving the problems besetting my hometown…Lynn Scoffetto's phone number and a picture of 343 B Street.

Chapter Sixteen

"That's crazy. None of this makes sense. Maybe you made a mistake. The address was wrong or you got the name wrong." Ruby's voice mirrored my own frustration and fear.

"Nope. I called the State Superintendent of Schools while I was still at Mom and Dad's house. He'd never heard of Onagitchee Children's Home."

"The court has been sending children to the school for over a year. What is going on?"

"I don't know, but I'm going to find out. For Cindy's sake and the other children who've been sent to this mysterious school. Maybe I'll confront Judge Oldham after I get home, demand that he tell me the truth." My arms sprouted goosebumps at the thought of the persnickety, slightly creepy, man. I'd always thought something wasn't quite right about him.

"I'm not sure that's a good idea, Indie. Maybe we should find out more. You can't just accuse a judge of doing something wrong without evidence."

"I've got to tell someone. They can't send any more children to a place that doesn't exist. Who knows where those poor kids have gone?"

"Okay, wait until you get home. I'll do some checking into the school tomorrow. You give me a call when you're back, okay?"

After saying goodbye, I dug the cell phone charger out of my purse and plugged it in beside the bed. I was only a couple of hours away from home, but after almost driving into the ditch, sleep became a priority. One more night in a motel and one more pizza delivery dinner.

I sat in an uncomfortable chair at a tiny table by the window, chewing a slice of overcooked cheese pizza and watching traffic. A police car drove by with lights flashing and no siren. *The strange events started the night I fell onto Winston Oligite's dead body and then, became more complicated the night of the storm. The shooter, finding Cindy's body. Hey, girl, don't forget Peter's help that night. He showed up right after the shooting stopped...*

I dropped the remainder of the pizza slice into the box. *Right after the shooting stopped. No, it couldn't be. Peter would never...* A sudden vision flashed through my mind. Peter's smile as he gazed down at the woman leaving his apartment; his look of contentment as he leaned over to kiss her goodbye. *Don't be ridiculous. Peter would never betray you.*

A sliver of moonlight crept between the curtain panels as I turned off the bedside lamp and crawled into bed. The pale, silvery light imparted an eerie, sinister appearance to the bland room. Shadows loomed over the bulky dresser and darkness swathed the open closet. I pulled the blanket over my head and fell asleep, wishing all bad things would just go away.

****

I arrived home the following morning to discover that the cleaning and repair companies had done a superb job. My home office looked pristine and the house held only the faintest trace of smoke smell. Amazing. I wandered into the garage and found a small stack of items rescued by the firemen. Sorting those could wait.

After several cups of coffee and a shower, I dressed in clean jeans and headed to the office. Ruby had a divorce trial in two days and she'd asked me to attend as her paralegal. Mostly because she needed someone to keep track of her multitudinous exhibits, the one thing she couldn't seem to do well.

I spent several hours labeling and indexing the exhibits, ensuring that I could instantaneously locate requisite documents during the hearing. Emotions run high during a divorce and people tend to fight over money. In this case, there was more than enough money and property for both parties to live comfortably for the remainder of their lives, but they continued to fight. Shaking my head at the foibles of the human race, I locked the now-organized exhibits in a file cabinet and called Peter.

To my astonishment, he answered on the first ring. "Hello, Indie. Back from your parents?"

"Yes, but while I was there I learned something I think you'll want to know."

"What?"

"Ah, this time I want information in exchange for my information."

"Indie, don't try to hold me up. You know I can't do things that way." He sounded indignant.

"And don't try to bamboozle me. What I've learned is astounding, frightening. You need to know, but I have a few questions of my own."

"Okay, give me what you've got and I'll do my best to answer your questions. Within reason."

I could hear his reluctance and suddenly, I knew how he must look. Brushing back a lock of that dark hair, his brow furrowed with exasperation, those brilliant green eyes clouded with doubt. A lump formed in my throat and I had to admit it—I missed him. Shaking my head to rid myself of the vision, I tried to steady my voice. "I want all the information you've got about Cindy's death. Do you have an autopsy report?"

"Yes, but it's harsh, Indie. I'm not sure you want to hear it."

I swallowed the lump in my throat. "I probably *don't* want to know, but I think I have to hear it. Something's very wrong around here and I think Cindy's death is the key."

"You may be right. Okay, there is no gentle way to say this. Cindy was raped and then, strangled." His voice sounded pained and full of sorrow.

I suspected as much, but it still hit me like a slug in the gut. *That poor, troubled girl. She needed and deserved help, but look what she got. The legal system failed her and so did everyone around her.* The sick feeling in the pit of my stomach grew.

"Are you okay? Indie? You still there?"

Fighting back a sob, I answered in the calmest voice I could manage. "Yes, I'm here. Pete, I want you to find out who did this. I want to know what the hell is going on around here. And here's something that might help." I explained what I'd seen at 343 B Street and then, gave him Lynn Scoffetto's name and phone number.

"I'll let you know what I find out." Again, he paused. "I'm sorry about Cindy and …"

"Yes, I know. Goodbye, Peter." I did know. He didn't mean to hurt me. We cared deeply for one another, but maybe we'd never been in love. Who knows? It didn't really matter now because it was over.

I drove home, letting the Camaro soothe me.

With a cup of coffee brewing, I carried my laptop to the kitchen table. The setting sun cast a warm glow through the window and gave me a cozy, safe feeling. It was time to organize what I knew, try to make some sense of everything that had happened.

Opening a spreadsheet program, I entered dates and events, watching for a pattern to emerge. I stared at the last entry, the discovery that no school existed at 343 B Street, and sipped my coffee. Nothing. Too many disjointed facts and unrelated dates. Too many deaths without a connection. What was I missing?

Winston Oligite died in the courthouse. Cindy Brodan died in the woods outside town. Gerry Marner died at home. There must be a connection. If not, it meant three killers roamed our little town and I couldn't accept that. I had to find a common thread.

It came to me the next day as I sat in the courtroom, handing exhibits to Ruby.

My mind had wandered in an attempt to forget the unpleasantness of the divorce hearing. Each party, acrimonious and vengeful, fought to make life miserable for the other. As a couple, they had done well financially, but dividing their lives and assets equitably proved difficult with both determined to "win."

With a bang of his gavel, Judge Oldham declared a ten-minute recess and told the attorneys to talk some sense into their clients. Attorneys and clients headed for the conference rooms down the hall. I remained in my chair, rearranging exhibits and wishing myself on a sandy beach or a mountaintop. Anywhere besides a courtroom.

That's when the answer popped into my head. The courthouse. All the victims had some connection to it. Cindy Brodan had a juvenile case handled in this building. Same thing with Winston Oligite's son. Gerry Marner...hmm, more of a stretch, but he did date someone who worked here. *What association could possibly exist between three murders and the courthouse?*

I leaned back in my chair and looked around the courtroom. Tall, narrow window flooded the room with sunshine, illuminating the oak-paneled walls and hardwood floors with a soft, golden glow. The jury box, unused during this hearing, held comfortable, padded chairs covered in dark green leather. At the front of the room stood the judge's bench, an imposing structure designed to instill respect and awe in judicial participants.

Respect and awe…I snorted as I thought of Judge Oldham fussing with his shirt cuffs. It was easy to see him in the role of medieval dandy wearing lace and slapping someone with a glove. Trying not to grin at the vision of the judge sporting a huge hat topped with a giant feather plume, I turned to the sounds of commotion at the door.

The attorneys and clients had returned. Ruby settled herself in the chair next to me. Her client, seated on her other side, brushed blond bangs from her flushed face and opened her mouth. Ruby gave a slight shake of her head in a mute plea for silence from her client, who appeared on the verge of eruption.

The hearing ended in moments. Although neither party looked happy, both had agreed to the settlement, including the appointment of a Guardian Ad Litem to safeguard the interests of the couple's children. The attorneys accompanied their clients out of the courthouse, probably hoping to prevent a physical altercation between the angry, soon-to-be-divorced litigants. Ruby's client, Judy Rothweil, stomped off in a huff when Judge Oldham hailed Ruby in the parking lot.

"Ms. Langdon, please get the Rothweil divorce decree to me for signature before Friday. I'm leaving this weekend for a two-week vacation." Judge Oldham extended his arm and peered at his shirt cuff, rotating his arm to view its entirety.

Ruby nodded.

The judge made a minor adjustment to his shirt cuff before turning his attention to me. "Hello, Ms. Stevens. I was sorry to hear of your house fire, but happy to learn you'd survived."

Okay, in a small town everyone knows everything that happens, but still… *Why would anyone tell a judge about my travails?* "Thank you, Judge. How did you hear about it?"

He stared down his nose and waved an elegantly manicured hand. "Oh, you know, people talk. Well, I must be off. Ms. Langdon, please see I receive your document in a timely fashion."

I pushed my glasses further up the bridge of my nose and watched Judge Oldham cross the parking lot.

"What was that about?" Ruby clutched her briefcase in one hand, glanced at her watch and then gazed at me.

I opened my mouth to answer, but the perky, inquisitive look on her face reminded me of one of those cutesy meerkat photos and I giggled.

"What's so funny? C'mon, Indie, knock it off."

"Sorry. You looked like something from a kid's poster."

She shook her head and rolled her eyes. "Honestly. By the way, thanks for doing such a great job in the courtroom today. I'll never understand how you keep track of so many exhibits."

"Organization, my dear, organization." I looked at Ruby, sophisticated and perfectly coiffed, and then glanced down at my own khakis and blue shirt, knowing my hair had yet again escaped the confines of my hair clips. "Hard to believe, huh?"

Ruby laughed just as my phone rang with its usual classical melody. She mouthed goodbye and waved before climbing into her car.

I glanced at the caller ID on my phone. "Hey, Anita. How are you?"

"Fine, fine. I wanted to invite you to dinner tonight. Steve was supposed to call you yesterday, but I guess he never got around to it. He and Brady were busy at Gerry's house, trying to dig out some of those huge weeds around the side."

"Dinner sounds great. Did Brady get an offer on the house?"

"No and he's convinced it's because the outside is such a mess. Several lookers, but no takers. So Steve hauled all my gardening tools over there and forgot my shovel."

I could hear the kids raising a ruckus in the background. "The kids home sick today? Sounds hectic at your place."

She groaned. "Yes, neither of them went to school today, but they both feel better right now and they're bored."

"Hey, do you want me to stop at Gerry's and pick up your shovel on my way to your house?"

"Really, Indie? You wouldn't mind? It would save me a trip in the morning. I'm not sure Steve will have time after work. At least not if I want him home in time for dinner."

"Don't be silly. Of course, I wouldn't mind. It's on the way."

"Bless you. Okay, dinner around seven. Be prepared for lots of 'the future of the band' talk."

"Okay, see you then. Thanks, Anita." I grinned at the thought of either of the guys pontificating about the 'future of the band' before I remembered Gerry's death necessitated the conversation.

"Oh, hey, hang on. Steve said something about digging out a drain in the basement, too. So if the shovel isn't outside, look in the basement. There's a key under the doormat."

"Sure thing. See you tonight."

I drove home and spent some time practicing the violin before I headed to Steve's for dinner.

Anita and Steve's house was in sight by the time I remembered my promise to stop at Gerry's for the shovel. *Plenty of time to go back without being late. Anita wouldn't complain about my forgetfulness, but she's so busy...*

After checking for traffic, I spun the Camaro in a neat U-turn and headed back to Gerry's house. Even though the sun hadn't set, the place looked dark and spooky. Trying to shake off my illogical uneasiness, I searched all around the outside of the house and inside the garage, hoping in vain I wouldn't need to go inside.

Figures. Now I have to go inside the damned place. Why can't guys put things away? Stomping all the way to the front steps, I retrieved the key from under the doormat and opened the door.

Even vacant houses are never silent. A soft breeze rattled a loose window. Water gurgled in a pipe somewhere. The refrigerator kicked on with a loud click and hum. As I tiptoed across the living room, the floorboards creaked. The basement door screeched as I swung it open and the hairs on my arms stood up.

When I flipped the light switch, a dim bulb barely illuminated the rickety wooden steps, leaving most of the room in murky shadow. I patted my pocket to make sure I had my cell phone and then crept down the stairs, keeping one hand on the wall. The boiler kicked on as I reached the bottom step and my heart made a wild leap. *Stop being ridiculous. Steve and Brady have been down here. Nothing is wrong or they'd have seen it. Get the damned shovel and go.*

I inhaled deeply to steady my nerves and the damp, musty air made me wish I could hold my breath. *Aha.* Something tall and thin leaned against the stack of cardboard boxes I remembered from my earlier visit. I took two steps toward the shovel and walked right into a thick cobweb. Now, I'm not afraid of spiders, but that slightly sticky, hair-raising feeling of a web glued to my face proved too much when coupled with the spooky ambience.

In an unreasonable panic, I danced around, swiping at my face, trying to rid myself of the gossamer strands. My elbow caught the shovel, knocking it to the floor and I tripped over the handle. I crashed into the stack of boxes, sending them flying and raising enough dust to choke me. Something sharp gouged my arm as I fell. Not a serious wound, just a small trickle of blood.

Well, if the outward expression of the inward harmony of the soul defines gracefulness as William Hazlitt said, my poor soul must be in chaos. I lay still, taking stock of my wounds and considering myself fortunate that nobody could see me lying on a dusty floor surrounded by crushed boxes. Gradually most of the aches and pains subsided and I pushed myself into a sitting position.

I tugged my (thankfully) undamaged phone from my pocket and turned on the flashlight app. The bright glow revealed a sharp slice down my forearm, not deep enough to be worrisome, just enough to smart. Pointing the phone light downward, I searched for my glasses and found them next to a small latch.

So that's what cut my arm. A couple of tiny blood drops glistened on the edge of the latch. *Weird...it looks like a door latch, but why put a door latch be so close to the floor? You can't even see it, unless you're clumsy like me and fall on it.* I knelt to look at the crazy thing and gave it an idle flip.

To my astonishment, a section of the wall slid aside.

Chapter Seventeen

A small room lay beyond the opening. Evidently, someone had gone to a great deal of trouble to soundproof the room because I recognized the material as the same I'd seen in a recording studio the band had once used. A mattress lay on the floor in one corner, complete with sheets and a fuzzy blanket. A couple of empty juice boxes, a grimy teddy bear and a pile of dirty clothes.

I switched off my phone's flashlight app and turned on the camera. Careful not to touch anything, I took photos of everything; the scattered boxes, the latch, the wall open and closed, the contents of the room. I stepped into the room and using the flashlight app again, I located a light switch near the ceiling.

The single bulb, nearly hidden inside a wire mesh cage, cast a sad glow over the already forlorn little space. I took a few more photos before backing out and flipping the latch. The ringing of my phone startled me as I watched the wall section slide shut, hiding the room from view.

"Indie? Did you forget about dinner?" Anita sounded amused.

"No, no. I just found your shovel. Be there in a few minutes."

"Okay, Steve's got steaks on the grill. He said to tell you to get your butt over here or the guys will eat yours."

"Yeah, yeah. On the way." I laughed. "*With* your shovel."

My appearance created quite a stir when I arrived at Steve and Anita's house.

"Oh, my God, Indie, what happened to you? Come on. Let's get this cleaned." Anita gasped and grabbed my arm, gently prodding the wound.

"I tripped in Gerry's basement. I'm fine, although I did lose a hair clip somewhere." I'd been so relieved to get out of the spooky house I hadn't considered how I must look covered with dust and the dried blood on my arm.

"I've hair clips galore and you're welcome to whatever you need. C'mon, you can borrow clean clothes if you want to shower. By the time you've finished, the steaks will be ready."

After steaks grilled to perfection and a long discussion, Steve, Brady and I agreed to disband the band, so to speak. Although Gerry's drinking had often impeded our practice sessions and occasionally ruined public performances, his murder shook all of us. A winter off would do us good.

"That doesn't mean you should be a stranger." Anita hugged me as I left in borrowed clothes.

"Thanks, Anita. I'll bring your clothes back later this week." I drove home slowly, thinking about the room. *Why would Gerry have a hidden room in his basement? It couldn't be old and forgotten because one of the open juice boxes still contained juice. I forgot to tell Brady about the room. Well, maybe he knows. If not, I can tell him later. Probably not important since he's selling the house.*

I parked the Camaro in the garage and headed straight for the coffee pot. Inhaling deeply of my favorite aroma, I took my filled mug and cell phone into the office and turned on my laptop. Using a data cable, I downloaded the photos from my phone to the laptop.

I scrolled through a couple of photos. *If you put shelves in there, it would be a great storage room for home-canned stuff.* I snorted at the thought of me canning anything. *Sounds like something mom or her friends would say. I must be getting old and domesticated. Time for another cup.*

After the coffee brewed, I splurged on calories with a bit of creamer before wandering back to my laptop, sipping appreciatively. *Bedtime for old ladies.* I poked at the power button, missed it and, instead, hit something that enlarged the current photo. *Whoa—what's that?*

I put my cup on the desk and slid into the chair. Using the editing program, I enlarged one area of the photo and took off my glasses to peer closely at the screen. No doubt about it. That pile of dirty clothes held something unexpected and the implications were frightening.

I stared at Cindy Brodan's t-shirt, the one she wore the last time I saw her alive.

****

"You must be mistaken, Indie. That doesn't make sense." Peter sounded exasperated and tired.

"Maybe not, but I know what I'm talking about. It's Cindy's t-shirt in the photograph. Come see for yourself." I felt instant aggravation and maybe even a little hurt. Here I was trying to help the guy, give him information about evidence that might relate to a terrible crime and he treated me like some crazy old lady who spied on her neighbors and called the fire department to get her cat out of a tree.

"Can't you just email the pictures to me? I need to get some sleep."

"Sure, but if you're not interested, I could call Shawn or one of the other guys." My face felt hot and I forced myself to loosen my grip on my phone.

"No, don't do that. Send them to me. I'm sorry, Indie. I'm just tired." He sounded wide-awake now.

"Fine, I just hit send. Call me back if you want to know more." Only slightly mollified by the apology, I poked the "End Call" button and stormed into the bedroom to change into pajamas. The phone rang just as I poked a foot into a pajama leg. Hopping around on one foot and grabbing for the phone, I managed to knock a book off the bedside table and the pillow off the bed.

"You were right. I'm sorry." Peter sounded contrite.

"I didn't notice it when I was in the room, but I saw it as soon as I used the zoom on the photo."

"I recognize it, too. She wore it the last time I saw her. I was the officer chosen to drive her halfway to Onagitchee to meet

184

the school's counselor, who picked her up." Peter's voice held a new note of strain.

"I don't understand how this could've happened. Doesn't anyone investigate facility credentials before ordering a juvenile transport? What's going on?"

"Those are questions I can't answer right now, but believe me, I *will* find out. You said these things were in a hidden room in Brady's house? The one Gerry willed to him?"

I nodded though I knew he couldn't see me. "Yes, but I don't think Brady knows about the room. I didn't mention it to anyone."

"Can you get Brady's permission for me to enter the house? I'd like to keep this as quiet as possible. If I don't need a search warrant, it'll keep the attention to a minimum."

"I'm sure Brady won't mind if I go into the house and I'll just take you along with me. Let me give him a call and I'll call you right back."

"Thanks, Indie."

****

I met Peter outside Gerry's house the following morning and lead the way to the basement. "See? There's the latch."

Peter's eyes narrowed as he watched the wall slide open. "How did you find this?"

My face grew hot and I hoped the dim lighting would hide my blush. Who wants to look like a klutz in front of an ex-boyfriend? Especially one who dumped you for a pretty homemaker type. "I tripped over a shovel and fell. Cut my arm on the latch."

He grinned and chuckled. "You are the only person I know who literally falls onto clues."

I moved closer to the open wall. "I don't believe it. Dammit. Somebody got here first." Someone had stripped the room of its contents. No clothing, no juice boxes, no teddy bear. Nothing but a mattress, sans sheets.

Peter swore softly. "Who else knew about this?"

"Nobody. I didn't even mention it to Brady."

"Okay, Indie. Go home. Don't talk about this to anyone. I need to get a team in here."

"A team? You mean Muley and his gang of evidence suppressors?"

"No. Listen, I can't talk about it. Just do it, okay?" His voice was hard, but his eyes held a pleading look.

"Yeah, sure, but when this thing is over, I want the whole story. See ya." That sad, vulnerable stuff works on me every time.

I drove to the office and checked my calendar. Yep, paperwork to prepare for Ruby's court hearings tomorrow. After reading two voluminous files of information provided by Child Welfare Services, or CWS, I prepared a summary of the facts in each case for Ruby's two new juvenile clients.

The younger client, an orphaned eight-year old boy, repeatedly ran away from the children's home where the others constantly bullied him. The second client, a thirteen-year old girl named Lula, had shoplifted a box of toaster pastries from a local grocery store. The store manager contacted CWS because the poor girl was starving. Her parents had departed for parts unknown, leaving the child alone in a house without utilities or food.

Shaking off a sad and gloomy feeling at the thought of these unloved and unwanted children, I made copies of the summaries for Ruby and then dialed her cell phone.

"Hey, what's up?" She sounded unusually chipper for a day before juvenile hearings.

"Wow, you sound happy. Win a big case today?"

"No," she laughed. "Actually, I got to spend the day at home with the kids today. We've been baking cookies."

"Sorry for the interruption. Give Amy and Tommy a hug for me."

"Don't be silly. You know you're always welcome here. Besides, I think more dough was eaten than baked."

I grinned at sound of the kids' chatter in the background. "I finished the summaries for your two new juvies tomorrow. You want me to run them over?"

"No, don't bother. I'll be over early tomorrow to pick them up. You could come over for a cookie though."

"Thanks, but I've got things to do. Are we still on for dinner this weekend?"

"That's next week. This Saturday Mark and I will be at his sister's graduation in Seattle, remember?"

"What? Are you sure?" I peeked at the calendar on my desk. "Woops, you're right. Your mom keeping the kids?" A loud bang made me jerk my ear away from the phone.

"Sorry about that. I've got to go." She sighed. "The kids just knocked an open bag of flour and two cookie sheets off the counter."

"Okay, see you tomorrow." Trying not to giggle, I hung up.

****

The next morning Charley Winslap called to ask if I had time to proofread two briefs.

"Sure. I can pick them up on the way to the office. I have to meet Ruby in half an hour, so I can stop by on the way."

"Great. Thanks, Indie. See you in a few."

After a quick shower, I tugged on a t-shirt and jeans and headed out the door with a travel mug full of my favorite brew. Charley seemed out of sorts when I arrived at his office.

"Here are the briefs." He handed me a thick envelope before fidgeting in his chair.

"Okay, when do you want them finished?" I watched him leap from his chair to pace across the room.

"Huh? Oh, whenever. No rush. A couple of weeks will be fine." His cheeks flushed a faint pink.

"What's wrong with you? Do you feel okay?"

"What? I'm fine. Hey, I ran into a friend of yours, Shawn Trellicki. He says you and Peter Hampton are no longer an item."

He flopped into his chair and picked up a pen, tapping it on the desk.

Puzzled, I stared at him. *Charley gossiping?* "Shawn isn't really a friend, more of an acquaintance. He's Peter's partner."

"Is it true?" He straightened in his chair and stared at me, no longer tapping on the desktop.

"Of course, they've known each other since high school."

He grimaced and shook his head. "No, not that. Is it true you and Hampton are no longer an item? Trellicki said Hampton is engaged."

"Yeah, sure, it's true. Why?" *Engaged after a few weeks? We practically lived together for three years, but we were never engaged. Ah, that's your own fault, my girl.* I stared at Charley, seeing the flush in his cheeks and the way he clenched his hands. "Charley, are you trying to ask me out?"

"I wondered about…no, that's…maybe," he spluttered, throwing himself into his chair and leaning forward to rest his elbows on his desk.

I couldn't help laughing. The terror of the office looked like a schoolboy caught with his hand in the cookie jar. I liked Charley. Always had. "Well, ask away."

"This is ridiculous. I haven't dated in years. Not since Marta and I divorced. Oh, forget it. I'm no good at this stuff." He looked at the ceiling, at the floor, anywhere and everywhere, except at my face.

"As my mother used to say, practice makes perfect." I grinned at him.

"Fine, dammit. Indie, would you like to go to dinner with me?"

"Not bad, but you need to be more specific." I reached over to pat his beet-red face.

"You aren't going to make this easy for me, are you?" He scowled, giving me his king-of-the-office look and, when I didn't flinch, burst into laughter. "Okay, how about this weekend?"

I left his office with a date for Saturday night and a grin on my face.

Chapter Eighteen

The blaring of Beethoven's Fifth startled me from a deep sleep. I fumbled for my glasses and nearly fell out of bed, grabbing the corner of my nightstand to save myself from crashing onto the floor. Teetering on the edge of the bed, propped up only by one arm, I succeeded in grabbing the phone only to lose the battle with gravity. I slid onto the floor and my flailing arms banged the nightstand, knocking off a glass of water, a book and sundry items.

Ignoring the still-ringing phone, I disentangled myself from the sheets and searched for my glasses. I found them, one lens cracked, under the edge of the bed. After drying my face with the bottom of my t-shirt, I slipped on the glasses and checked caller ID on my phone. *What in the world would make Ruby call so early?* I dialed her number.

"Hi, Indie. I thought you might still be sleeping."

I grinned as I glanced at the book I'd spread open to dry and the sodden sheets on the floor. "Not anymore. What's up?"

"I have a favor to ask. Could you keep Amy this weekend?"

"Sure, but I thought they were staying with your parents. What happened?"

"A friend invited Tommy to a weekend camping trip and I know the parents well, so it's just Amy. She was supposed to stay with mom and dad, but Mom isn't feeling well. I think she has that flu that's been going around. I'd take Amy with us, but there are no seats available on our flight."

"Stop worrying. I'd love to have her."

"Thanks, Indie. You know how Mark hates to go to these things alone and he's so proud of his sister that I'd feel terrible if he missed her big day."

"Okay, call me later with details. Like when you want to bring her over, that sort of thing."

"Thanks, Indie."

I laid down the phone and surveyed the chaos in my bedroom. *Time to clean the mess. Nah, not just yet.* Grabbing the damp blanket from the floor, I climbed into bed, pulled a pillow over my head and immediately fell asleep.

Beethoven awoke me again several hours later. This time I managed to pick up the phone without disaster. "Hello?"

"Good morning, Indie. I realized last night that I hadn't said when I'd pick you up. You haven't changed your mind about dinner, have you?" Charley sounded nervous.

"No, but..."

"But?"

"Well, Ruby called earlier and asked me to keep Amy this weekend. I'm sorry, Charley, but I guess I'll have to ask for a rain check."

"Nonsense. Children have to eat, too, you know." His voice held a bit of the office ogre.

I laughed—an anxious schoolboy one minute, decisive man the next moment. "Are you serious? You wouldn't mind?"

"Of course not. Ruby and Mark have raised terrific children and I enjoy their company. I'll pick you both up at seven, okay? No, wait. That's too late for a child to eat dinner. How about five?"

"Perfect. I'll see you Saturday." I ended the call and sat on the edge of the bed, thinking. His concern for Amy startled me, but I liked the way he looked after the child's well-being. Too bad nobody looked after the children sent to the Onagitchee School. *Don't state laws require schools be accredited? If so, there should be a list of acceptable facilities. Who is responsible for keeping the list updated?*

I waited for state offices to open to embark on what proved to be two hours of fruitless phone calls. The out of state program was so new that nobody seemed to have a clear idea of who did what, but all agreed somebody had to vet every facility. Finally, a faceless voice had an answer. Sort of.

"No, ma'am. I can't give you a name. I can only tell you that it's a part-time worker. Our regular employees are just too busy to keep track of little details."

"Who *could* give me a name? Please transfer me." " I shook my head. *Little details? Part-time workers are verifying the quality of juvenile placement facilities?*

After twenty minutes and countless transfers, I learned the "quality control" person had a second job at the courthouse. Nobody knew the name of the part-time employee because the person in charge of that department had left on vacation and her records existed only on a password-protected computer.

Gritting my teeth, I showered, dressed and drove to the courthouse. I spent a frustrating hour wending my way from office to office, asking subtle questions about part-time jobs. Finally, I climbed the wide, oak staircase to the Clerk of Court office.

"Good morning, Mrs. Hofstedder." I learned long ago that Clara preferred a formal approach. She considered a lack of formality as bad manners.

"Good morning, Miss Stevens. How may I help you?"

"I'm looking for information. Would you know of anyone who works full-time in the courthouse, but also has a part-time job?"

She gestured toward the row of desks where her deputies sat. "I'm sorry, Miss Stevens. As you can see, all of my positions are filled. You're welcome to fill out an application, but I'm afraid I have no openings at present."

"I beg your pardon, but I guess I didn't make myself clear. I am not seeking a job. I am trying to find the name of the person who works part-time for CWS verifying facility information. Checking school accreditation, complaints, that sort of thing."

"I'm sorry, Miss Stevens. I know nothing of such things, but maybe one of my girls... Do any of you know anything that might help?" She turned toward her deputies, eyebrows raised.

Four deputies shook their heads. The fifth, grouchy Gloria, glared at me through narrowed eyes.

"Thank you for your help, Mrs. Hofstedder."

"Good day, Miss Stevens." She returned to her desk.

I glanced at the row of desks as I left the office and felt a shiver creep up my spine at the sight of Gloria's malevolent scowl.

****

Friday rolled around and Ruby knocked on my door promptly at three o'clock.

"Come in, come in. How's my favorite little girl?"

Amy's smile sparkled. "Aunt Indie, I brought you a present."

I knelt to her eye level. "You did? What is it?"

"It's a surprise, so I can't tell you. You have to wait until later. It isn't good to have dessert before dinner."

I laughed and ruffled her hair. "Okay, Miss Smarty-pants. How about you put your bag in the spare bedroom?"

She bounced out of the room, dragging two pink duffle bags behind her.

"You look beat. How about a cup of coffee?" I looked at the dark circles under Ruby's eyes and motioned for her to follow me to the kitchen.

She plopped into a chair while I made coffee. "A quick cup, maybe. I've dropped Tommy at his friend's house, but I still haven't packed. These two new juvie cases are kicking my ass."

I stared at her. In all the years we'd been friends, I'd heard Ruby swear once twice; both times while she was in labor and I'd driven her to the hospital to await Mark. The second time it had been close with Mark arriving from a faraway customer site just as the hospital staff wheeled her to the delivery room. "What's so difficult about the new cases?"

"Both neglected children and Judge Oldham has ordered both of them held in state custody."

"State custody where?" I had a feeling I knew what was coming.

"He's sending them both to Onagitchee, saying it's for the children's safety." She held out a hand for the coffee mug and then, slumped forward, leaning her elbows on the table.

"How can he do that? I thought that out of state program was for delinquent children, older children."

She shrugged and shook her head. "I don't know what's going on. I asked the judge to reconsider his order, to let the children go to a local foster home. I felt so strongly that I offered to care for them myself."

"Wow. How did he take that?" I was flabbergasted. Attorneys just don't do such things.

"About the way you'd expect. He stared down from the bench and said he'd hold me in contempt if I didn't stop talking. What could I do?" She looked so woebegone that it nearly broke my heart.

"Well, I might have a lead on what's going on with that school." I explained about the part-time CWS worker. "But, I haven't had any luck finding a name."

Ruby drained the last of her coffee and put the mug in the sink. "Maybe I can help with that. When I get back from Seattle, I'll call a few friends and see if I can find a name for you."

I gave her a hug and pushed her gently toward the door. "Okay. Right now, you try to forget all this and go have fun with Mark. Amy and I will have a good time. Hurry up or you'll miss your plane. By the way, Charley is taking Amy and me to dinner tomorrow night."

Eyes wide, Ruby turned to stare at me. "A date with Charley? Mr. Lord of the Office actually asked you out?"

"Hey, he's a nice guy. He–"

"Just giving you a hard time. Besides, I knew he asked you out. He told me." Ruby laughed and gave me a friendly poke in the shoulder.

Amy and I spent a great evening eating pizza and watching animated movies streamed to my television. She slept on the floor in her sleeping bag and I fell asleep on the couch. I woke early and lay snuggled under my blanket watching her sleep. A small, blond curl lay across her forehead and her chin rested on her tiny hand. *Kids…so sweet, so innocent.* Before I waxed maudlin, Amy's eyes popped open.

"Is it time for breakfast, Aunt Indie?"

"You betcha. Name yer poison, girlfriend."

"I don't want poison. I want pancakes."

"As Your Highness wishes." I curtseyed and exited to the delightful sound of little girl giggles.

After breakfast and dishes, we filled the day with a trip to the library, a dip in the local pool, lunch at the Sandwich Shoppe and a cartoon matinee.

"Okay, time to head home. There's just enough time to get us both ready to go out for dinner." I buckled Amy's seatbelt over her booster seat before starting the Camaro.

"With Charley, huh? Mom says you like Charley, but he's a boy." She giggled.

"Boys aren't all bad, you know." I grinned at her. "You think we might get cooties from poor old Charley?"

She contemplated the question. "Nah, Charley is too old for boy cooties."

I laughed and drove home.

Chapter Nineteen

I had just finished tying a pink bow around Amy's ponytail when I heard a car pull into the driveway. I glanced at the wall clock. *He's early.* A horde of fluttering butterflies invaded my stomach. *Don't be silly. You've known Charley forever.*

In her frilly pink dress, Amy bounded past me and flung the door open, calling, "Charley!"

It wasn't Charley. It was Peter, looking gravely handsome in his deputy sheriff uniform.

"You're not him." Disappointment showed on Amy's face.

Peter gave Amy one of his fetching smiles. "Hi, Amy. No, I'm not Charley. Did you and Indie get ice cream today?"

Very primly, Amy lifted her eyebrows and straightened the hem of her dress. "No, we haven't had our dinner yet."

"Go get your sweater, Amy. It's almost time to leave." I couldn't help smiling –she looked like Ruby admonishing one of the children.

Peter watched her dash toward the spare bedroom and turned to me. "Who is Charley?"

I tried not to melt under the gaze of those bright green eyes. "Nevermind. Did you need something?"

"Yes. Well, no." He looked confused, befuddled. "I, uh, came to give you news about the Onagitchee School."

I waited without speaking.

After a moment, he stepped further inside, closer to me. "Listen, Indie, I miss you. I mean, she's a wonderful girl…"

I shook my head. What a mess we'd made of our relationship. Maybe it had always teetered on the brink of disaster and I'd never noticed. "Don't do this, Peter. It's over. Now tell me about the school."

A vulnerable, hurt look crossed his face before he straightened and stood tall. "Yes, I wanted you let you know that Onagitchee is under interdiction. No children will be sent out of state until a full investigation has been completed."

A silver SUV turned the corner and stopped in front of my house. "What about the children sent earlier this week?"

His eyes widened. "This week? Damn. I knew nothing of this. From our local court?"

"Yes, two of Ruby's clients." The SUV door opened and Charley climbed out.

"Good evening, Indie." Charley held his hand out and shook hands with Peter, eyeing his uniform. "Everything okay?"

"Fine, fine. Peter stopped by to give me some information about a case. Thanks for letting me know, Peter." I tried to keep my expression neutral, but he knew a dismissal when he heard one.

Those amazing green eyes flashed with something unreadable, but he didn't argue. "Goodnight, Indie. Nice to see you, Charley."

"You ready to go?" I closed the door behind Peter and turned to Charley. The butterflies in my stomach disappeared at the sight of his easy smile.

"Yep. Where's Amy?"

I found her in the spare bedroom where she'd been so distracted by a new book we'd bought earlier she'd forgotten about dinner. I grabbed her sweater and book while Charlie led Amy outside. He installed the booster seat and we all headed off in the SUV.

Though the crisp days of fall offered fewer hours of daylight, it was light enough to see cars nearly filled the restaurant parking lot. The riot of laughter and chatter made it difficult to hear the greeter's voice as he seated us and proffered menus. Not a rowdy joint, just crowded.

Seated beside me, Amy lifted her eyes from her book only to ask for a grilled cheese sandwich. Charley raised his eyebrows and I shrugged, laughing. Only a kid would ask for a grilled cheese sandwich in a place like this.

Linen tablecloths and napkins, intricately carved wood-paneled walls, deep plush carpet, subdued lighting from crystal chandeliers, wide windows offering a view of the placid lake. I declined to peruse the wine list and ordered coffee with a seafood platter. Charley chose the same and then turned to me.

"Have you started editing the briefs?"

"No, I thought…" A loud burst of laughter from a crowded table in the furthest corner interrupted me. I was surprised to see

Judge Oldham and his wife Minnie seated at the packed table with Sheriff Muley, Shawn Trellicki, a deputy attorney from the county attorney's office, several CWS people, and Gloria, the deputy from Clara Hofstedder's office. Quite a distinguished crowd.

"Must be the power table. Wonder what's going on." Charley grinned and rolled his eyes toward the corner. Two waiters carried in a large cake complete with lit candles and placed it in front of Judge Oldham, unknowingly answering Charley's question.

As the group burst into a loud version of "Happy Birthday," it drew even Amy's attention. She lifted her eyes from her book and said, "That's a bad man."

Startled, I stared at her. "Who is a bad man, honey?"

She pointed at the Judge. "He has cake and he isn't sharing with us. Mommy says everyone should share."

Charley leaned forward to pat Amy's head. "He is sharing with his friends. See?"

She nodded, but cast occasional glances toward the corner where a waiter cut and served cake to the judge's guests.

After he finished cutting cake, the waiter carried a tray to our table. He placed a slice of cake in front of each of us. "With Judge Oldham's compliments."

I smiled and waved at Judge Oldham and the others at his table. To my astonishment, Amy clambered down from her chair and carried her saucer to the next table, where a small boy sat with his parents. At his nod, she cut her cake in half and slid half onto the boy's plate before returning to her chair with her own smaller portion. The boy's mother shrugged and smiled at me.

Next to me, Charley muttered, "From the mouth of babes."

Taking a cue from Amy, I gave my cake to the boy's parents to share. The judge whispered to the waiter, who cut the cake into smaller pieces and passed them out to smiling patrons. Charley handed me a fork and pointed at his slice of birthday heaven, grinning. Amy chattered as she ate her cake, oblivious to the small stir of goodwill she'd caused.

On the drive to my house, she fell asleep in the back seat. Charley glanced in his rear view mirror. "Nice kid."

I smiled, thinking of Amy marching to the next table to share her cake. "Yes she is. Ruby has done a fine job with both her kids."

"I like kids. Liz never wanted children. Said they were an inconvenience." The dash lights illuminated Charley's face, revealing a sorrowful expression.

I'd only met Charlie's former wife Liz once, but once had sufficed. Perfect hair, expensive clothes and an attitude of disdain for everyone around her. "Was that why you divorced?"

"In part." He glanced toward me as we pulled into my driveway. "It also had something to do with her running off with Mitt Howard."

"Mitt Howard? The guy who owns that big oil company?"

"Well, to be precise, it's the guy whose *father* owns a big oil company, but I guess that was close enough for Liz." He grinned and shut off the SUV engine. "It's worked out well for her. Jet setting around the world without responsibility. I've been over her for years, but do wish it had happened sooner. Probably too late for me to have children."

"Don't count yourself out. You're still young enough to have kids."

"You propositioning me, Ms. Stevens?"

I could feel my cheeks burning and hoped the blush wasn't visible in the dim light. "Huh. Not me, soldier. I have enough to do getting this one to bed." I jerked my thumb toward Amy, now stirring in the back seat.

"Here, let me carry her to her room."

I unlocked the front door and followed him inside. By the time I'd helped Amy into her pajamas and tucked her under a snuggly fleece comforter, Charley had coffee ready.

"Perfect." I sniffed my cup with appreciation and sipped. "Thanks."

He nodded as he took a seat across the table. "Nothing beats a good cup of coffee."

"Ah, a man after my own heart." *Damn. Why can't I learn to keep my mouth shut?* Thankfully, Charley didn't seem to notice.

"So did Muley and his gang figure out who trashed your office?" He got up to refill our coffee mugs.

"I haven't heard a word. Nothing about who tried to burn my house down. Nothing about any of the weird stuff going on in this town."

"Listen, Indie. I don't know what's going on either, but be careful. I've felt something brewing for a long time." He glanced at the cup in his hand and shrugged, grinning. "No pun intended."

"I'll be careful. I promise." I walked him to the door after he finished his coffee.

He pulled his keys from his pocket and stared down at the floor. "Uh, what do you say to a, uh, real date? I mean, just two, uh, just us?"

I looked at him. Really looked at him. Blue jeans, pale blue shirt, dark blazer. A great looking guy with that graying hair and lean build. "Charley?"

He lifted his eyes to my face for only a moment before returning them to my fascinating carpet. A faint, red color spread over his face. "Yes?"

"I'd love to go on a real date with you."

He exhaled and spoke in a rush. "Okay, I'll call you tomorrow. Thanks for a terrific evening." A hurried kiss on my cheek before he was out the door and gone.

With a grin on my face, I closed and locked the door before peeking through the curtain to watch the SUV drive down the street. I grabbed a book and headed for my bedroom, stopping at the guest room to check on Amy. The hallway light spilled into the room, dimly lighting her angelic face and chubby fist tucked beside the pillow. I picked up her teddy bear from the floor beside the bed and laid it next to her before tiptoeing across the carpet to close and lock the window.

****

I awoke with a start. You know that creepy, crawly feeling you get when something's not right? Like someone is sneaking up behind you. Nothing you can see or hear, but you know you're in danger. That's the feeling I had as I rolled my head from side to side in the dark room, looking for an intruder, but saw nothing. Not even an unexpected shadow. I slid sideways off the bed, twisting my body to land on my knees with a muffled thump.

A muffled thump…made me think of another night, not so long ago. The night Winston Oligite died. His murder had sickened me, but, perversely, also saved me. He…

The slight sound of a cracking shrubbery branch pierced the veil covering my sleepy brain. With frightening clarity, I realized someone stood right outside my window. My heart pounded and my chest labored for breath. Oh, God, not now. Not tonight while Amy slept in the room next to mine. Amy. All alone in the dark and vulnerable. I had to get her and take her to a safe place.

Breathing deeply and willing my heart to quit pounding loud enough to break the nighttime noise curfew, I grabbed my glasses and crawled to the door. I didn't want to give my stalker a chance to see me. If anything happened to me, Amy would be alone and helpless.

Sliding my hands and knees forward so I wouldn't make thumping noises, the ten-foot journey to the guest room lasted forever. Or, it felt that way. Finally, my shoulder banged into the bed frame and I stretched out my arm, trying to find Amy by touch. No sleeping angel, so I lifted my head with reluctance.

Snowy white sheets gleamed in the bright moonlight spilling across the empty bed. Amy was gone.

Chapter Twenty

A second sharp crack and a muffled moan sounded near the window. I leaped to my feet and bounded across the bed to the window. It stood open, the mangled screen discarded on the lawn. A dark shadow, clutching a small bundle with blond hair, darted around the corner of the house and disappeared. The roar of a car engine dissuaded me from jumping through the window to follow.

Instead, I ran to my bedroom to snatch up my cell phone and car keys from my bedside table before sprinting to the garage. The Camaro awoke with a mighty growl. *Thank God for Mr. Yenko.* Slamming it into reverse, I hurtled onto the street in time to see taillights in the distance, racing toward the edge of town.

The speedometer hit one hundred before I reached the end of the street. Where was a cop when I needed one? Even if the clunky local police cars couldn't keep up, it would be a comfort to know they were behind me. I grabbed the phone from the passenger seat and tried to dial 911. Too shaky, too distracted. I couldn't even hit three little numbers without taking my eyes from the road. The phone rang as I tossed it to the floor on the passenger side.

One hundred forty. The engine topped out by the time I hit city limits, but no matter. I was gaining on the taillights. They disappeared around a corner, but I knew where to turn. Only one road crossed the highway at that spot. I eased off the accelerator as

I approached the curve, but it wasn't quite enough to keep the rear tires from sliding as they crossed from pavement to gravel.

Silently blessing my father for teaching me to drive in all condition, I corrected automatically and slammed down the gas pedal as the car moved into the turn. It skidded onto the straightaway with roar of joy. Released from all restraint that beautiful 427 rose to the occasion, screaming down the gravel road in pursuit of Amy's abductor.

With tears streaming down my face, I followed the taillights through the sparsely populated sections of the road. *Who the hell is driving that car? Who knew Amy was at my house? Did a random peeper spot her through the window?* Impossible. I knew I had locked the window and closed the shades. Hadn't I?

Beethoven burst forth from somewhere on the passenger side floor. I ignored it and concentrated on the car in front of me, terrified that if I lost it I'd lose Amy forever.

The gravel road narrowed. I'd followed the unknown car deeper into the rural area than I normally traveled. Few houses lined this road, the homes all separated from one another by empty fields interspersed with wide sections of dark, brooding forest. Farm country. Early to bed. I hadn't seen a single lit residence since leaving the main highway.

My cellphone rang again. I couldn't reach it without stopping the car and fishing around on the floor where I'd tossed it and so, I let it ring.

The car in front of me slowed and the Camaro moved closer, prompting me to reach for the headlight switch. It was possible, although unlikely, the driver hadn't noticed me following. If he saw my headlights, I would lose any element of surprise.

Surprise? Whatever happened, I'd be as surprised as the driver would because I had no plan. Pushing my glasses higher up on my nose, I considered my options. The Camaro had definitely gained ground and I'd soon be near enough to ram the vehicle, but a collision might injure Amy. Should I turn off the headlights? No. If I drove off the road, nobody would know Amy needed help. What to do? No idea, but first, I had to catch them.

A minute later, I knew catching the car would not be a problem. I could see the taillights turn onto a subsidiary road. Only one house lay at the end of that turnoff. Judge Oldham. Judge Beecher freaking Oldham. Impossible. Unbelievable.

I had a sudden vision of the Judge pursing his lips as he fussed with his shirt cuffs and lectured from the bench about propriety. More than one attorney had squirmed at the courtroom lectern as the Judge pontificated, usually about some minor, imaginary infraction. I remembered the condescending look on his face tonight as he motioned for the waiter to share birthday cake with the restaurant patrons.

I disliked the man from the first moment I met him, but is he mixed up in the abduction of a child? It didn't seem likely. Yet, his orders sent all those children to a nonexistent school and he knew Amy was with me because he'd seen us at dinner.

The Camaro throttled down with a touch of reluctance when I eased off the accelerator. I had the feeling the car enjoyed running flat out, but it certainly hadn't done any favors to the gas gauge. Crossing my fingers for luck, I gave a silent plea to the gods of gasoline to hold out a little longer.

The car ahead reached the crest of a hill and the taillights winked out. Rolling down the window, I heard the muted roar of the river and a loud gurgling as it rushed over a boulder near the bank. I flipped the headlight switch off and hoped the noise of the water would mask the sound of the Camaro's engine.

Darkness enveloped me, setting my nerves on edge until I thought I might scream. Even with the moon shining brightly overhead, I could barely see the road. My speed slowed to a crawl. Somewhere ahead a car door slammed.

I pulled the Camaro onto the shoulder of the road and searched for my cell phone. *Damn. Dead battery.* I tossed the phone on the seat and slipped out of the car, nearly panicking when the dome light came on automatically. No one seemed to notice. At least nobody showed up with a gun, which was good enough for me. I said a silent prayer of thanks and stepped out.

The moment my feet touched the gravel surface I realized I'd forgotten something important. I had no shoes. After a few steps on the sharp pebbles, I knew a change was in order or I wouldn't make the quarter mile to Oldham's mansion.

Thank God for flannel pajamas. They tear easily, especially old ones. I ripped fabric from the knees down and used it to wrap my feet. Not exactly a fashion statement, but it helped. Halfway up the hill, something sharp sliced through my left pajama-shoe. It burned and stung and hurt with that odd sensation that comes only from stepping on glass. Every movement was agony. I bit my lip to keep from crying out and tried hopping on my right foot.

It didn't work. I landed face first in the gravel, adding a bloody face to the mess of my feet. Lifting a hand to my cheek, I felt glass shards. Just my luck to walk barefoot on glass and then, fall face first on a broken bottle. *What's next...stinging nettles?*

I tried to pull the slivers from my face, but succeeded only in driving them deeper. Alone in the dark, I whimpered, wishing for someone, anyone, to appear and whisk Amy and I away.

Amy. The thought of her drove me to my feet. I staggered and stumbled forward in the moonlight. The hill proved steeper than I expected and the backs of my calves began to ache. I could feel the glass move deeper into the flesh of my sole. One foot in front of the other. Up and up.

Just when I thought I could go no farther, I heard voices. The words were indistinguishable, but the tone was argumentative. I thought of all the detective shows I'd watched and vaguely remembered it was smart to lower your profile. People tend to stand watch by looking at head height for intruders. I crouched and crept forward on tiptoe, but that pulled the muscles tight across the sole of my foot. That piece of glass, or whatever it was, sawed across the stretched muscles like a fiddle bow sawing across catgut strings.

Tears streamed down my face and my eyes rolled. I was losing it. Mostly definitely losing it. *Get yourself together, woman. Amy is depending on you.* I set my shoulders, gave up on my effort at surreptitious surveillance and hobbled around the last curve in the road.

A gleaming white car stood in driveway, one of the rear doors hanging open just far enough to activate the dome light. Its dim beam revealed a heavy mesh screen between the front and rear seats. I could just make out the shadowy shape of a telltale red light on the car roof. A police car.

I'd followed a deputy sheriff car from my house to Judge Oldham's home.

The only deputy who knew I had Amy was...no, I don't believe it. Not Peter.

Something heavy slammed into the back of my head and the world disappeared in blackness.

****

Voices woke me, but barely. My head throbbed and my eyes wouldn't focus. I knew I must have a helluva of concussion. However, that paled in comparison to the agony of my sliced and bloody foot. When I tried to shift my position to ease my bruised and aching body, I discovered someone had bound my hands and feet with duct tape. Even worse, I knew whoever had done this to me had Amy.

214

"What are we going to do with her?" The second voice was female and somehow familiar, but I couldn't quite place it.

"That's a decision for the boss, not me. I recommend a quick bullet to the brain followed by a trip to the dump. I have no problem doing it myself if the boss wants it done. Hell, if that damned Steve and Brady hadn't showed up at Marner's place, I'd have shot the stupid, interfering bitch right then and we wouldn't be having this problem." Shawn spoke nonchalantly.

"I don't want anything to do with murder. This other, it's bad enough, but it pays well. Nothing pays enough for murder."

The boss…it had to be Judge Oldham. Why else would we all be here? Why had Shawn and this mysterious woman taken Amy? Shawn and Peter had been partners for many years. A feeling of dread began in my stomach and moved up to my chest, squeezing the breath out of my lungs. *Peter saw Amy at my house tonight. He's the only one who knew, besides Charley. One of them must have tipped off the 'boss' about Amy's whereabouts, but why?*

The silver tape across my mouth prevented me from screaming, but I couldn't help moaning. If I managed to escape, an unlikely proposition at best, whom could I call?

Who will help when there's no difference between the good guys and the bad guys?

Chapter Twenty-One

"At least get her out of here, can't you?" The woman's voice turned snide. "Unless you need orders from the boss before you can wipe your own butt."

"Watch it, Gloria, or you might end up as the one with a bullet in the head." Shawn's not-so-subtle threat gave me goosebumps.

Gloria? Gloria. Gloria Smith, Gerry Marner's cousin. Clara Hofstedder's deputy clerk. No wonder she sounded familiar.

"Don't even think of touching me. The boss wouldn't like it. You know we're very close." Gloria sounded almost as menacing as Shawn.

"Oh, I know it and it sickens me. Both of you sicken me."

Gloria is "close" to Judge Oldham? I tried to imagine the two of them together, but it didn't work. His obsessive, fastidious grooming. Her narrow, mean eyes. The pounding in my head wiped out the vision of Oldham fussing with his shirt cuffs.

"What I do is none of your business. Now get her out of here."

Footsteps moved across the room and stopped by my side. Shawn peered into my eyes. Never a very handsome man, anger now twisted his facial features, imparting an almost demonic look.

The little piggy eyes narrowed and he licked his lips before he spoke. "Awake, huh? You know, I never liked you. Always snooping around, sticking your nose into everyone's business. I never understood what Pete saw in you, but I guess he had his reasons."

I squirmed, trying to inch away from his hungry gaze.

He laughed and grabbed my chin, squeezing so hard tears filled my eyes. "Oh, yeah. I think me and you are going to have a good time."

I wanted to spit in his face. I wanted to scream at him, hit him, but the duct tape made all those gratifying actions impossible. Trying to wriggle away made me feel weak and pathetic, so I gave it up and glared at him.

"Oh, good. I like a woman with a bit of fire. I hope you like it rough because I do." His hands moved down my body, stopping to caress my breasts before he leaned over and ran his tongue across my cheek.

I tried to quell the nausea I felt at his touch. With tape covering my mouth, vomiting didn't seem like a good idea and I had a feeling neither of them would help me.

"Knock it off, Romeo. Get her out of here. You'll have time for that later." Gloria's voice held a smug note of authority.

I sensed Shawn's barely contained anger as he stood and yanked me by the arm, pulling me to my feet. Pain rushed over me, blanking out all thought, leaving me weak and shrieking without sound. My knees gave out and I sagged against Shawn.

"For Christ sake, this is one of the reasons I hate women. Stupid, whimpering bitch. Stub your toe and you fall to pieces."

Gloria laughed with a horrible gritty sound. "I don't think it's a stubbed toe. Look at the blood pooling there. Get her out of here, you effing idiot. Put her in with the others. The boss is going to be pissed about the mess on the carpet. Cover up that foot."

He looked around for a moment and then, pulled a plastic liner from a small trashcan. After shoving my foot into the bag, he watched my face as he jammed his thumb against my sole.

The chunk of glass inside my foot slithered further upward and I felt myself losing consciousness. I was only vaguely aware that Shawn picked me up and carried me to another room. When he tossed me onto the concrete floor, I passed out for a second time.

I drifted back into the world under protest. *It hurts. Go away. Leave me alone.*

Something nudged me, gently at first and then, with more insistent. Trying to roll away from whatever or whoever it was, I groaned and willed myself back to never-never land.

Nudge, nudge. Poke, poke.

I gave up trying to make myself disappear down Alice's rabbit hole and, instead, turned my head to the source of my irritation. Darkness swathed the room, nothing visible except a tiny slice of light glowing beneath the door. *I love you, photons.*

My thoughts weren't rational and I knew it, but I wanted to know who lay beside me. I tried jerking my head toward the glow, but my head had wedged against the wall. The person beside me seemed to understand and he/she wiggled toward the door.

Even in the feeble sliver of light, I recognized the eyes and blond hair. *Amy.* I felt a sob build in my chest and stifled it. Nodding my head, I tried to indicate to her that I wanted her to move away from the door and get behind me. I could do little or nothing to protect her, but at they'd have to move me aside. It would give her an extra moment to live.

Listening for any change in the continuous bickering between the two imbeciles in the next room, I began chewing the duct tape covering my mouth. After gnawing and spitting for twenty minutes, I'd freed enough of my mouth to start chomping on the tape binding Amy's hands.

When I finished, Amy immediately pulled at the silvery stuff holding my hands captive. We sat, rubbing our numb wrists and ankles, for several minutes before she put her mouth close to my ear to whisper. "I want to go home, Auntie Indie."

"I know, sweetheart. Just be quiet and let me think."

"Auntie Indie, I think they hurt that boy over there." Her soft, sweet voice quavered and my heart ached with the thought of the terror she must feel.

"Stay here and be brave, sweetie. I'm going to check on the little boy, but I'll be right back." I crept across the room on my knees to spare my battered feet further indignity. Besides, I didn't want to step on anyone and provoke a reaction that might alert our captors.

There wasn't only one little boy.

There were three children, although in the darkness I couldn't tell boy from girl. I satisfied myself that all three were breathing and had a pulse, but I knew I couldn't remove their bindings. A scream or shriek from a frightened child was sure to bring Shawn Trellicki bounding into the room and I knew he wouldn't hesitate to kill one or all of these children.

I could do nothing except whisper reassurances into each child's ear, encouraging them to remain calm and comforting them with the thought of rescue.

Only I knew that nobody would help. No one knew these children and I were here in the basement of Judge Oldham's house. If I had a phone, who could I call? The police? We already had one sheriff's deputy on the premises, but he wasn't here to help. I had no way of knowing how many deputies might be involved and the judge himself must know of our plight because Gloria and Shawn expected him to arrive soon.

Feeling utterly disconsolate and helpless, I crawled back to Amy and cradled her in my arms. She patted my cheek with her tiny hand and I knew she trusted me to do something, to help not just her, but the other children, too.

I had no weapon to use in defense of these little ones and no phone to use to call for help. Assuming the entire justice system wasn't involved in this nightmare. Hell, I couldn't even turn on the light switch to ease a child's natural fear of the dark.

Well, I could go down fighting. It might not help, but I had to try. I tugged Amy toward the corner where the other children lay weeping silently. Little Amy helped me move them close together. She patted their heads and whispered to them in her tiniest voice.

I stationed myself in front of them, determined to hold off our captors as long as possible. Weary beyond description, I dozed off and awakened when the door flew open with such force that it slammed into the wall and a bright, overhead light blinded me.

Trying to shield my eyes, I struggled to stand. Shawn Trellicki jabbed the barrel of his gun into my ribs with such force it made me gasp. *Bruised ribs. One more thing to add to the litany of my miseries.* Beside me, the children whimpered through their taped mouths.

"Hey, lookee here, Gloria. The stupid bitch got herself un-taped." He drew his arm back and punched me in the stomach.

My abdomen cramped and my vision blurred, but I still saw the sudden flash of blond hair leaping in front of me. Amy shrieked as she kicked Shawn in the shins and grabbed for the gun. "You leave Indie alone!"

"No!" The shout burst forth from my throat like the roar of a lion, surprising even me.

The gun boomed and a chunk of ceiling fell to the floor. Shawn pushed Amy, knocking her down. Her head bounced once as it hit the floor and she lay motionless, unconscious. "Get back, you stupid little snot. God, I hate kids."

"You bastard. I swear I'll kill you if you've harmed her in any way. Amy, are you okay? Amy?" I staggered to my feet, reeling like a drunken bum.

Her little body remained motionless. Shawn snorted, "Forget about her. Now, get out here. Nice and slow like so I don't have to shoot you and mess up the nice carpet."

"Let them go. Please, Shawn. I'll stay. I promise. Just let the children go home."

"Seems to me you don't have much choice about staying. Don't worry about the children. They will all be going home. To a new home, anyway."

"What are you talking about? What new home? What the hell is going on here?" I heard the near-hysteria in my voice and knew my breaking point fast approached.

He laughed and gestured with the gun. "You won't be around long enough to worry about it. Just shut up and walk nice and slow into the other room."

"Not until I check Amy." Knowing he planned to shoot me gave me a perverse sense of well-being. At least I knew what to expect. My feet were giving up the attempt to hold me upright anyway. I dropped to my knees and brushed the hair from Amy's forehead.

Her breath came softly, rhythmically and her pulse felt strong. She probably had a concussion, but she was alive. Relief flooded through every tense muscle in my body.

"Come on, Shawn. Quit screwing around and get her out here. I heard a car a minute ago. I think the boss is here." Gloria sounded excited. "I can hardly wait to see what the boss will do with *her*."

With a last glance at Amy, I hobbled and staggered to the next room. Every step shifted the glass in my foot and provoked a new round of bleeding, which I saw without feeling. My body had taken such abuse I no longer felt pain. I figured that wasn't a good sign, but what the hell. At least I could look around the room instead of struggling to remain conscious.

The place was creepy. The judge might live in a mansion, but his basement looked like everyone else's. Unfinished wood beams holding the floor above served as the ceiling. Cobwebs festooned the corners and shelves filled with canned goods lined the walls. The damp, musty air and strange odor made the hair on my arms stand up. For reasons I couldn't fathom, someone had spread a beautiful and expensive rug over the concrete floor and arranged a chocolate brown leather sofa stood beside it. A weird déjà vu feeling came over me each time I looked at the rug.

A door upstairs opened and slammed. Gloria smiled and jigged around as she spoke. "Here comes the boss. Oh, this should be good."

A heavy tread sounded above us. Another door opened with a squeal and the rickety stairs creaked as the Judge approached. My heart pounded and my lips felt so dry that I couldn't open my mouth. *How could he? All those years on the bench...all those children shipped off to a phony school. So much misery. People trusted him, believed in him, and he betrayed everyone.*

The pounding in head grew unendurable and my heart beat so fast I thought it might explode.

With a thump, he landed on the bottom stair and stepped around the corner.

Except it wasn't a he. The boss wasn't Judge Beecher T. Oldham.

Chapter Twenty-Two

Minnie Oldham, in all her matronly glory, stared at me. "What the hell is going on here?" Her eyes held a dangerous glint and she spoke with a hard edge in her voice.

Gloria's smile faltered. "Hi, boss."

The menacing glance softened and Minnie leaned forward to give Gloria a peck on the cheek. "Hello, dear. We'll talk later. Right now, I want to know what's going on. Did you get the Langdon kid? Why is *she* here?"

"Yeah, I got the kid. Snatched it from *her* house." Shawn jerked his head toward me. "That's why she's here. Stupid bitch followed me."

Minnie's face turned bright red and she slapped Shawn's face. "You effing idiot. Incompetent fool. How could you let her follow? What if someone saw her?"

A deep ruby handprint formed on Shawn's cheek. He clenched his jaw and narrowed his eyes. "Nobody saw her. There's nobody on the road. I'd have got rid of her already, but your girlfriend there wanted me to wait for you."

"Watch your mouth, Trellicki. There are plenty who can replace you, you know." Minnie turned to me.

An aura of menace engulfed me and I'd have sworn the temperature in the room dropped twenty degrees. I stared at her, this past-middle-age woman. She wore her soft white hair piled in a conservative bun and the flesh under her chin jiggled when she shook her head. Her lacy, pink cardigan didn't quite close across her huge bosom.

She conspicuously looked me up and down, laughing aloud when her gaze reached my feet. "My God, you're a mess."

Green and blue flannel pajama bottoms torn off at the knees, a bedraggled t-shirt, filthy, blood-encrusted feet wrapped in strips of dirty fabric. She was right…I made a real fashion statement. "Thanks. How kind of you to notice."

She slapped me, hard enough to make my ears ring. I was getting used to it. *Hell, I'll probably never know I'm awake until someone hits me.* The absurdity of the thought hit me and I couldn't stop a grin from spreading across my face.

"You're a real smart ass, aren't you? I hope you can find something to laugh about when you die. Shawn, take her outside and shoot her. Make sure you gag her first so her caterwauling doesn't alert half the county. When you finish, throw her in the river."

I lunged forward, hoping to scratch her damned eyes out or at least get in a few licks before they took me out. Despite her bulk, she was quicker than I'd expected. She darted aside and I fell, missing her lifeless eyes, but leaving a wide bloody scrape across her cheek. She tripped and landed on top of me crushing the breath out of my lungs. I felt a rib or two crack. The sharp, stabbing pain in my chest elicited only a moment's surprise. Every part of my battered body hurt so badly that one more whack just didn't matter.

She clambered to her feet and grabbed a handful of my hair, yanking me up. I swayed and stumbled as she jerked me across the room to where Gloria stood, watching and licking her lips. "Would you like to help Shawn dispose of her, dear?"

"Oh, yes, please. I wanted nothing to do with murder, but I've decided to make an exception in her case, the stupid bitch." Gloria glared at me and then, grabbed Shawn's arm. "Let's go."

"Hold on. Before you two head out for your little session, I want to see the kids. How many besides the Langdon girl?" Minnie let go of my hair and I dropped to the floor, unable to stand.

Shawn shifted his weight from one foot to the other. "Three. Two boys and a girl. Slight problem, though. The Langdon kid fell on that concrete floor in there and hit her head. She's still unconscious."

"Fell? You shoved her." Gloria could scarcely contain her malicious glee.

Minnie pulled a tissue from her cardigan pocket and dabbed at her cheek before turning furiously to Shawn. "If you've damaged the kid, I'll kill you myself. She's our biggest moneymaker, a custom order. Bring them all out here."

Shawn left and returned carrying a weeping Amy, who hung limply from his arms. She had regained consciousness and stared with frantic eyes at the man holding her. Shawn must have un-taped the other three children because they, wide-eyed and clutching one another, followed behind him.

"Amy." I managed to maneuver myself to my knees before Minnie reached out with an expensively shod foot and shoved. My head connected with the corner of a table behind me and a horrible, sharp pain shot straight through me. My vision swam and I felt a trickle of blood down the back of my neck.

"Let me go! Let me go! I want Auntie Indie."

With blurred vision, I dimly perceived Amy struggling with her captor. She kicked and twisted, pounding at his face with her hands while she shrieked.

"Oh my God. Incompetents surround me. Put her down, you idiot. She's not going anywhere." Minnie heaved a great sigh that made her massive bosom quiver. She jerked her head at Gloria, who stationed herself next to the stairs.

Amy ran straight to me and helped me sit. My vision wavered in and out, but I felt better with her close. The other children scooted past Shawn to stand behind me. Too battered and weak for coherent thought, I leaned against the offending table for support and spread my arms in a pointless effort to protect all four.

With a derisive snort, Minnie nodded at Shawn. "You and Gloria take the snoop and get rid of her. Make it fast and get back. You must deliver these four tonight or the sale is off. The usual routine; bound and gagged in the trunk. Gloria knows where to go. I'll take care of the merchandise while you take care of Stevens."

Custom order? Merchandise? My God, the Judge's wife is involved in child abductions. "What do you mean by custom order?"

Minnie laughed. "You think everything is spur of the moment, luck of the draw? You're as much of an idiot as my husband is. No, you little fool, this operation requires delicate and careful planning. It's true that we auction casual merchandise to the highest bidder, but our real profit comes from custom orders. We photograph likely candidates, provide the photos to buyers and collect the child for delivery when our price is paid. That reminds me...Gloria, we'll need a new photographer now that Gerry is no longer with us."

"Gerry was your photographer?" My stomach heaved as I remembered the box of photographs in his closet. It made sense in a sick way. *My God, the broken guitar pick I'd seen in the shrubs when I took Ruby's kids to the park...it was Gerry trying to lure Amy away. Probably hoping for a bonus.*

Footsteps sounded on the steps, treading carefully one stair at a time. A peevish voice called out. "Dear, are you down here? What are you doing in the base... Oh, I'm sorry. I didn't know you had company." Judge Oldham stopped in the doorway, brushing imaginary lint from his jacket sleeve.

"Go back upstairs, Beecher. This doesn't concern you. Leave. Now." Minnie wheeled to face her husband.

The judge bristled at her threatening tone. "Now, see here, Minnie. You have no call to speak to me in that manner. It's my house, too, you know. In fact, my grandfather…" He turned to look at Gloria and Shawn, his eyes widening at the sight of the gun. When he looked at me, his eyes bulged. "I demand to know what's going on. My God, this woman needs medical attention and why are these children here?"

Minnie imitated the Judge's habit of fiddling with his shirt cuffs. "That's it, Beecher. I'm sick of you and your annoying, mincing ways. I've been hoping for an opportunity to rid myself of you and this seems like a good time. Shawn, take him with you and deal with him the same as Ms. Stevens."

"Am I to understand you are threatening me, Minnie?" Judge Oldham drew himself up to considerable full height and glared at his wife.

She laughed—a joyless, lifeless sound that made the hair on my arms stand up. "No, it isn't a threat. A simple statement of fact. Shawn will shoot you and throw your body in the river. Hm, I think it would be best to do him first. She's less likely to get away. Him first, her second. Gloria, help me tie His Honor while Shawn keeps him covered with the gun."

"Minnie, Minnie. What has happened to you? You were such a dear, little thing when we married. What the hell is going on? You don't expect me to cooperate in the ridiculous plan of yours, do you?" He jerked away from Gloria and the rope in her hands.

"Makes no difference to me. You cooperate or I'll have Shawn plug one of these brats. It will be worth the financial loss to see your face as you watch a kid's brains splatter the floor. That one should do." She shrugged and pointed a manicured nail at the smallest boy.

Stunned into obedience, the judge stepped forward with his hands held out. "No, wait. I'll cooperate. Tell me why, Minnie, why you are willing to kill me. What are you doing with these children? Why is Miss Stevens such a…a…such a mess?"

"I'm willing to kill you because I can no longer tolerate your namby-pamby, do-gooder ways. I want a life, a real life. I'm tired of being stuck in this shithole. I have money of my own now, lots of it. Tonight is the last delivery we make and then, I'm out of here. There. That should answer both questions. Wait, I forgot about Stevens. She looks a mess because she sticks her nose where it doesn't belong. Does that cover everything, Beecher *dear*?"

Beecher T. Oldham looked as if someone had punched him in the gut. He swallowed and closed his eyes. When he opened them, it was to gaze at his wife with steady, calm vision. "Take me, if you must, but let the others go. Miss Stevens has never harmed you and the others…my God, Minnie, they are *children*."

"Most of them are fated to end up in your courtroom and to spend their childhoods as wards of the state. A financial burden and a headache to everyone. Who will miss a few brats? Nor do I have any inclination to change my mind. Take him, Shawn."

Deputy Trellicki nodded and gestured toward the stairs with his gun.

Judge Oldham stared at him. "You are a disgrace to your uniform. Did you not swear an oath to uphold the law and protect citizens from harm?"

"So what? I lied. Not much different from anyone else in this county. Look at your own wife." He snorted.

Minnie's eyes narrowed. "Shut up, Trellicki or I'll give you a taste of *my* sharpshooting skills. Gloria, shove those kids into the back room and lock the door. I'll wait here with Stevens until you finish with him."

With poor Judge Oldham trussed up like a chicken and no white knight in sight, I knew I had to do something. The children remained close, leaning against my back. *Come on, just do it. You're no help sitting here and they are going to shoot you anyway. The old 'no guts, no glory' thing.*

Looking at each of the children in turn, I held a finger to my lips and then, struggled to my feet. Or to be more precise, my one undamaged foot. Blood continued to seep from my right foot and it hurt too damned bad to use it. I hopped a few steps nearer Shawn.

"Hey, what are you doing? Get back over there." Shawn waved his gun in my general direction.

"Please, let the kids go. I promise I won't tell anyone. Shawn, we've been friends for a long time. You just can't do this."

He threw back his head and laughed.

While his enjoyment of my plight distracted him, I launched myself at him. My head slammed into his abdomen and the gun went off, the bullet striking the opposite wall. He fell, somehow landing on top of me.

Through a haze of pain, I heard the screams of terrified children and the click of someone cocking a gun.

In a grim voice that gave me goosebumps, Minnie said, "Move out of the way, Trellicki. Ms. Stevens just bought herself a ticket to the promised land."

"Hold it right there. Drop the gun, Mrs. Oldham. Put it down nice and easy. Now move away from it."

Suddenly, the room filled with people and noise.

"You have the right to remain silent."

"Hands behind your back."

"Cuff her."

"Deputy Hampton, get those children out of here."

Hampton? What's happening? Where is..."Amy. Amy, where are you?" Like a dog that barks at the chain tethering him to one spot, I wept in frustration at my body's refusal to move. The pain in my head simply overwhelmed me, pinned me to the floor. *That's me, a butterfly on a collector's board.*

"Ma'am, lie still. The medics are on the way."

The room swam in and out of my wavering vision and I couldn't see the face behind the soothing voice. "I want to stand up."

"I think it best if you stay..."

"No. I want up. Now." I gritted my teeth and rolled onto my side. The sudden movement initiated a wave of nausea, but did relieve the pressure on the back of my head. "You win some, you lose some."

"Beg pardon, ma'am?"

"Nothing, nothing. Whom do you call when the good guys are bad? Mary had a little lamb, but that didn't help her." I couldn't stop the stream of nonsense flowing from my mouth.

"Get those medics in here. We've got a head injury." The soothing voice turned authoritative as fingers gently probed the back of my head.

"No, I'm fine. Only thinking aloud. Get me up." With a strength borne of idiocy, I managed to stand by grasping nearby arms and dragging myself upward. I knew immediately I should've listened to the paramedic. The pounding in my head warred with the throbbing of my foot, but nausea threatened to make the conflict irrelevant. *To the carpet, anyway.* I felt a grin spread across my face. "I think I'm going to throw up."

"Hang on to her. Don't let her fall." The unknown voice spoke and arms tightened around me. Sheer stubbornness kept me conscious.

"Sir, the stairway is too narrow for the stretcher. We'll have to carry her out." Another medic.

I tried to shake loose from the grasping hands. "Let me go. I can walk. Well, hop."

"Let me through. Dammit, get out of the way." A new voice spoke. Finally, somebody I recognized.

"Charley?" I tried to focus my eyes, but didn't entirely succeed. I saw two Charleys standing beside two Peters.

"Yes, I'm here, Indie. So is Peter."

"I know. I see all four of you."

Behind me, the medic voice spoke. "Double vision, probably due to the head injury."

The doubles merged into one. "Where are the children? Where's Amy?"

"They are outside, receiving medical attention. They are all fine, just thirsty and hungry. Let's get you out of here, ma'am." The medic smiled at me.

I shook off the hands supporting me and immediately collapsed forward. Charley and Peter both leaped to grab an arm. Laughter welled up. Strange, I know, but my daddy always told me there's something funny in every situation. Here I am, in a room filled with handsome uniformed men…me in my torn pajamas and no earrings. "Damn, I need a cup of coffee."

Charley laughed.

Peter frowned. "Indie, the last thing you need is coffee. You need the hospital and medical attention. Come on. Let me carry you up the stairs." He held out his arms.

I stared into those brilliant green eyes, remembering the dreams we shared and the years spent together. Peter is a good guy in his own way, but it's not my way. Somehow, he knew. He nodded and stepped aside.

Charley reached out to shake Peter's hand and then turned to me with his arms outstretched.

He swept me off my feet.

Chapter Twenty-Three

Outside, we discovered the ambulance had departed. The remaining paramedic apologized. "I'm sorry for the wait ma'am, but we had no idea all these children were here. They are uninjured, except for the bump on Amy's head, but the hospital has counselors, doctors and food waiting for them. I'll call for another ambulance right away."

"No, don't bother. I don't need one. Thanks anyway." I smiled at the medic from my secure perch in Charley's arms.

As Charley maneuvered me into his car, Judge Oldham called to us. The headlights of the nearest police car illuminated a bewildered, defeated man. His shoulders slumped, worry lines creased his forehead and he twisted his hands together, ignoring his disheveled clothing. "Ms. Stevens? Just a moment, Mr. Winslap. If I may, I'd like speak to you both before you leave. I want to apologize. I don't understand how I could have been blind to Minnie's extreme behavior, but I assure you I knew nothing of this."

"I know that, Your Honor." I spoke gently, afraid of shattering what little remained of the man I knew. Yes, the man I'd always disliked, but now pitied. After all, his wife's betrayal had destroyed his world and almost made him an accomplice to unspeakable crimes.

A tear glistened in the corner of his eye. "I will, of course, assume all responsibility for your medical bills and those of the children."

"Thank you, sir. That would be a help since I blew my savings on a car. Ah, my car...Charley, I left the Camaro parked down the road. Could you drop me off at the car and follow me home so I can put it in the garage before I go to the hospital?"

Charley glanced at my foot with its impromptu flannel bandage. "I think the hospital is first priority, dear. Besides, I don't think you'll be driving a stick shift for some time."

"Perhaps I might be of assistance?" The Judge stopped wringing his hands. "I planned to drive into town to stay at a hotel. I believe the federal agents wish to cordon off my home for some time. I'd be happy to drive your car to your home for you."

"Hey, thank you, sir. The keys are under the driver's seat, but how will you get to work and back here when they finish with your home?"

"I'll take a cab." A pained look crossed his face. "If you feel you can trust me sufficiently to give me access to your home, I will put the car in your garage."

"The house key is on the key ring. The garage remote is in the glove box." I squinted at him, realizing only then I'd lost my glasses in the brouhaha in his basement. A wave of nausea washed over me and my head started throbbing.

"Go, go. Get this woman to the hospital, Mr. Winslap. Don't worry. I shall take care of everything, Ms. Stevens."

I don't know if it had something to do with feeling useful, or if it was the thought of driving my hot Camaro, but the Judge appeared to be on the mend. He stood straight and tall, fussing with his cuffs as he watched us drive away.

Charley covered me with his jacket and I fell asleep the minute he started driving, waking only when the car stopped. The harsh glare of neon lights and the aroma of coffee prodded me into semi-awareness.

A man of his word. Charley had bought me a cup of coffee.

Chapter Twenty-Four

Charley refused to answer my questions until I'd slept, which I did.

I woke up in the hospital a day and a half after the fiasco at the Oldhams. I learned later than I'd slept thru multiple examinations as well as surgery to remove the glass from my foot.

Swimming back into conscious after absorbing enough anesthetic to knock out a Clydesdale is harder than you might think. The pounding in my head had subsided as had the agonizing pain in my foot, but I felt groggy. My vision was so blurred I reached automatically to push up my glasses and discovered I had none. I had a vague memory of breaking them, but couldn't quite remember how.

"Ah, Sleeping Beauty has awakened." Charley's voice came from a chair beside my bed. He kissed me on the forehead and placed something in my hand.

"Hey, where did these come from? Didn't I break my glasses? These look new." I held them close and squinted.

Charley plopped back into the chair and scooted it nearer my bed. "They *are* new, courtesy of His Honor."

I slipped them in place. "Judge Oldham bought new glasses for me? Wow, they're perfect. How did he manage that?"

"He called every optometrist in town until he found yours. That's not all he did. He chartered a private plane to fly Mark and Ruby home the same night I brought you here."

"Holy cow, that's all pretty sweet, but he can't keep doing that sort of thing. He wasn't responsible for what his wife did."

"He also hired a security firm to guard your house."

"What? Has he lost all his marbles?" Hunger replaced grogginess and I had trouble thinking.

"Listen, the nurse should be here in a minute. We'll talk more later, but just know this thing is bigger than we thought. The FBI wants us to keep the story to ourselves for the time being."

Mystified, I closed my mouth to forestall my questions and instead, watched the nurse bustle in carrying a tray. Cafeteria food, but I wasn't feeling picky. She sat the tray on one of those tables intended to fit a hospital bed and tugged the stethoscope from around her neck.

"Now, Miss Stevens, I need to check your vitals." She glared and pursed her lips. "If the gentleman would leave us for a few minutes."

"No, the gentleman stays." I returned the glare through my new glasses, trying to keep a straight face. Grumpy people always amuse me. Yeah, I'm weird that way.

Charley and I smiled at each other behind her back. I hadn't noticed earlier, but he looked tired. Beyond tired. Stubble covered the lower half of his face and his clothes looked rumpled as if he'd slept in them. "Hang on, aren't those the same clothes you wore when we went to dinner?"

He nodded and ran a hand through his hair.

Suspicion bloomed in my mind. "Have you been here the whole time I slept?"

He chuckled, but it had a weary tone. "I wanted to be sure you didn't make off with my jacket."

I gave him a withering look and waited for Nurse Grumpy to finish her business. She finally left, slamming the door behind her. Before everything in the room stopped vibrating from the shock, someone opened the door again.

Judge Beecher T. Oldham tiptoed into the room, carrying a bouquet of roses and a huge shopping bag. "May I come in, Ms. Stevens? If you aren't up to visitors, I thoroughly understand."

I was drifting, hunger forgotten, feeling the effects of whatever Nurse Grumpy had in her hypodermic, but I shook myself awake. Semi-awake, anyway. "Of course you may come in. Pull up a chair, such as it is."

The judge eyed the straight-backed metal chair and grinned. "Looks like the chairs we had in law school. I think they're designed to keep students awake."

"Do they work?" I laughed, though it set off another round of headaches.

"Occasionally. Mr. Winslap, would you do the honors?" He set the flowers on a table and handed the bag to Charley.

Charley peered into the bag and began laughing. "Judge, I had no idea you knew Indie so well." He bustled about near the sink, hiding his efforts by keeping his back turned to me.

A wonderful aroma soon spread throughout the room. I could scarcely contain myself. "Coffee! You brought me coffee?"

Charley held forth a cup filled with the nectar of the Gods

The judge beamed. "Not just any old coffee. This contraption can do everything from brew a cuppa to fold your laundry."

LEDs winked and the water tank hissed softly, heating in preparation for the next cup. I'd never seen such a fancy machine. "Judge, I appreciate everything you've done, but you've got to stop this. You are going to bankrupt yourself."

He helped raise the head of my bed just enough to allow me to sip without drowning myself. Waving a hand at Charley's offer of a cuppa, he scooted his chair closer. "Nonsense. My blindness allowed Minnie to take advantage of people. However unknowingly, I am the indirect cause of much suffering. I realize money cannot erase my culpability, but please allow me to atone in my own way."

Charley re-joined us, sipping from his own fragrant cup.

"Mr. Winslap, have you told Ms. Stevens the news?" The judge sat ramrod straight in his chair, no fiddling with shirt cuffs.

Charley yawned. "Sorry. No, didn't have time. The nurse just left."

"If I might make a suggestion? Perhaps you would like to go home. Take a nap and get a shower. That sort of thing." Judge Oldham laid a friendly hand on Charley's shoulder.

"A nap? No, I'm fine." Another giant yawn belied Charley's words. "I don't think Indie should be alone, at least not until the feds have picked up everyone involved in this thing."

"Mr. Winslap, I shall remain in this room to guard Ms. Stevens until your return. I will be diligent, I assure you. Besides, it isn't often I get to spend a day with a pretty young woman who is captive to my stories." The judge smiled at both of us.

"Go home. I appreciate all you've done, but I promise I'll be just fine." I patted Charley's arm.

"Well, if you're sure...I could use a shower."

"Yes, you could. Go on. Get some sleep. The judge can give me the scoop." I hammed it up, holding my nose shut with the hand not occupied with the coffee mug.

He leaned over the bed to kiss my cheek. "Okay, I'll be back later. To pick up my jacket, of course."

After he left, the judge made a second cup of coffee for me and I settled in to listen to the judge tell the story. "Now, remember I don't know all the details. Nobody does, but it *is* all confidential. I only know this much because the FBI needs all of us as witnesses, including you. I am telling you all this with their express permission providing, of course, you agree to confidentiality and to serve as witness."

At my nod, he continued. "You know suspicions were aroused by the multiple local murders and the disappearance of several children. It turns out a certain group of people were already being watched by the feds, suspected of participation in some sort of child porn ring. When your friend Peter went to the feds with information regarding possible malfeasance in the local law enforcement, (I think it started with the destruction of evidence, your car to be precise) the feds put it all together and didn't like what they saw. They recruited Peter, who acted on their behalf throughout this affair."

"So Peter was truly the person responsible for initiating the investigation here, in our county?" *And to think I suspected him of involvement.*

"Yes. If not for his efforts, Min…Minnie and her cohorts might have succeeded. Excuse me for a moment. I need a drink of water." He swallowed and looked down at the floor.

I felt only compassion for the man as I waited while he filled a glass with ice water.

He drained the glass and continued. "It turns out the group made a fortune, abducting children and selling them to the highest bidders in online, invitation-only auctions. Suffice it to say, none of the children sold have been found. The feds continue to investigate the group, trying to find all members, both sellers and buyers. Nobody knows how high up this goes. Locally, both private citizens and government officials are involved."

"Who?" My heart skipped a beat. *How many of my friends and neighbors were involved in this?*

"You know, of course, that both my wife and Deputy Trellicki were involved, as well as Gloria. Apparently, Gloria moonlighted for Child Protective Services as an investigator responsible for verifying accreditation for schools." He held up a hand. "Yes, there are rules against such things, as well there should be. Her double role in the system allowed her unprecedented access to extensive information."

"Oh, my God." I could barely breathe, imagining the horrible possibilities of the wrong person in such a position.

He closed his eyes for a moment before proceeding. "Quite. Now the clerk, Clara Hofstedder, appears blameless. Blind to everything going on around her, yet blameless, although the FBI will work to verify that before making a decision. I'm not sure of the names, but at least one deputy prosecutor appears to be involved. The feds have charged Sheriff Muley with destruction of evidence and assorted bribery counts. He had nothing to do with the child abductions, but did destroy your car in return for money. From my wife, of course."

It pained me to see the hurt look on his face. His recent behavior had changed my opinion of him. Despite his own horrendous humiliation, he did his best to help others and set things right, although some things couldn't be rectified. Like the murder of the Brodan girl. "Judge, have the investigators discovered who killed Cindy?"

"Yes, the bullet removed during the autopsy matched the bullet recovered from my basement ceiling. DNA tests prove Shawn Trellicki raped the girl, but there was a second assailant, as well. The FBI suspects Gerry Marner acted as Trellicki's partner, but the testing isn't complete. In face of insurmountable evidence, Trellicki confessed to the rape and murder, as well as the murder of Marner."

"How was Gerry involved in this? Was he truly the photographer as your wife said?" I began to feel faint, wondering how far the corruption had spread. *How can I live here, knowing I'll always wonder who might have escaped detection?*

"I'm sorry, dear. I know what a shock this must be to you. Shall we talk later? Perhaps you'd like to rest?"

"No, I think I need a glass of water. Please go on." I gulped the icy water, wishing it could wash away even some small part of my revulsion. "Okay, I'm fine now. Please go back to your story."

"Apparently, Gerry photographed children and occasionally used his basement to hide children. I believe someone in the ring discovered Gerry's predilection for child porn and blackmailed him into participation. His drinking became a liability when he gabbed too much, so Trellicki shot him and tried to make it look like burglary. Trellicki thought you might have seen him with Marner on the night of that big storm. That's why he tried to kill you."

I got a sudden chill, remembering the hidden room in Gerry's basement. "A picture of Cindy...I found a picture hidden in Gerry's living room."

The judge nodded. "Yes, Peter mentioned your discovery had led to Marner's link in the chain."

"What about Winston Oligite? Who killed him?" The scent of his aftershave had hung over me for days, despite numerous showers, and I shivered at the memory of feeling his dead body beneath me.

"I'm afraid that was...I'm afraid it was my wife." His eyes clouded and he began twisting his hands.

Stunned, I stared at him. I'd been sure the footsteps outside my office that night had been those of a man.

"It seems she wanted the Oligite juvenile files destroyed. She had a buyer for the boy and wanted him adjudicated a delinquent so the court would sentence him to the out-of-state 'school.' When you dug up information confirming the boy's innocence, Minnie realized an investigation might lead to me and thus, to her. She lured Winston to the courthouse and killed him there."

"But, why in my office?"

"I think that was coincidence. Your office was the only unlocked door Winston found when he tried to run."

Bizarre. Like an atomic chain reaction, forgetting to lock my office door led to breaking up a child abduction ring. I swallowed the sudden lump in my throat and shivered hard enough this time to make my teeth chatter. *It's all too much. I need to get out of here, visit my parents again or maybe sit on a beach in Hawaii. Anything, anywhere, but here, where the world is upside down.*

Like an automaton, Judge Oldham continued his litany. "Now, that deputy who works in the office downstairs…the nasty one. You know, the gossip queen…what's her name?"

"Rhoda Bellinger?"

"Yes, that's the one. She was involved in some way, although the feds haven't determined her role yet. She's the one who kept an eye on Marner and suggested he'd outlived his usefulness."

"Her own daughter's fiancée? My, God." I could no longer hold back the horror; I vomited, splattering my sheets and the floor. Too weary and appalled to care, I curled up on my side and closed my eyes.

The judge leaped to my bedside. "I apologize, Ms. Stevens. I've been terribly selfish. Telling the story to you has been my own catharsis, a way of sharing the burden. I apologize. Let me ring for a nurse."

"Wait. One more question, please. The school…all those women pretending to be teachers." I closed my eyes, wishing the room would stop spinning.

Judge Oldham snorted. "Yes, very interesting. It seems all those young women were actresses hired through a casting agency. Not one had an inkling of what really went on, except the supervisor. She is in jail in Pennsylvania, awaiting extradition. Like everyone else in custody, she is spilling her guts, hoping for a reduced sentence."

I was only vaguely aware of the nurse entering the room and chastising Judge Oldham for keeping me awake. Nurse (now not so) Grumpy sponge-bathed me and changed my sheets with the assistance of an aide. I swam in and out of consciousness too many times to help.

****

When the hospital finally released me to return home, federal agents had already arrested most of those involved. I'd heard rumors the connections ran to the top levels of state government, maybe even crossing state lines, although I'd read of no corroborating arrests.

Heartsick and weary of the whole mess, I took a cab home from the hospital, declining multiple offers of succor. I had something to do and wanted to do it alone.

I instructed the cab driver to pull into the parking lot in front of the courthouse, assuring him I'd make it home on foot. The crutch I carried slowed me down, but not by much. I sat on the bench where Rhoda had sat comforting her daughter. Rhoda, who had requested the murder of her daughter's fiancé. The crimes committed by those sworn to uphold justice had destroyed so many lives.

The imposing structure cast a shadow over the buildings across the street. I stared at the white stone façade, stretching above me five stories high. *Fiat justitia ruat coelom.* The words etched into the stone above the great wooden courthouse doors caught my attention. *Let justice be done though the heavens may fall.*

Cindy Brodan; the man who murdered her sat in jail, as did the parents who chose to sell her to the highest bidder. Justice done, but none could return the beautiful young girl to life. Nor could justice restore the loving husband and father to the Oligite family. How many unnamed children passed through the hands of those involved? Caught in the abductors' snare of greed and lust, most of these children had vanished without a trace.

Disillusioned and bone-tired, but determined, I peeked into the offices I passed as I hobbled my way to the basement. Though the faces smiled and nodded, I recognized few. The arrests at the completion of the federal investigation left most offices devoid of all but one or two employees.

The heavens had fallen in my small town.

Chapter Twenty-Five

Golden sunlight streams across the balcony where I lounge, easing the constant ache in my foot. Gazing across the sparkling blue of the Mediterranean Sea and holding a glass of exquisitely perfect iced tea, I know life doesn't get any better. Although some days I wonder…

Over two years had passed since I left the hospital. Many things changed after that day, but one that remained was my limp. It seems the large chunk of glass had worked its evil magic halfway through my foot, severing assorted muscles and tendons. I consider it a small price to pay for the lives of Amy and the other children.

The day I turned the key in my office door lock for the last time burns in my memory. I'd shredded all my documents and files, sold the Camaro, packed up my coffee pot and departed, never to return. To the county's dismay, I'd refused to surrender my grandfather's perpetual lease. Instead, I'd passed the lease to Charley as allowed in Grandfather's legally executed agreement with long-dead government officials.

Ah, Charley Winslap. A man fit to take on government corruption if ever such a man existed.

Next week would mark my two-year anniversary. Marriage proved my salvation and succor through recent sad events. To lessen my burden, my husband made the arrangements when my parents died in an automobile accident. He planned the lovely funeral service according to my parents' wishes, outlined in the copies of the wills they'd given me years ago, and he salved my hurt with a mountain of flowers.

He surrounded me with beauty and new friends when Ruby abandoned me. She could not forget Amy's abduction happened on my watch. Knowing I had locked the bedroom window and risked my life to save her daughter made no difference. She could neither forget nor forgive. During her sole visit to the hospital, she sat stiffly erect in her chair, unable or unwilling to meet my eyes. I had called her a few times, but she didn't return my calls or answer my emails. Mark neither visited nor called. I never saw Amy after the night at the Oldhams' mansion.

After I sold my little house, I left the town of my childhood and never returned. These days I split my time among the several homes we've purchased since our marriage. An elegant villa in Italy nestled within the rolling hills of Tuscany, complete with a small vineyard. A tiny cabin in the Swiss Alps where it pleases me to keep a small herd of goats. A lovely flat in London near Hyde Park and my favorite shops.

Our most recently acquired, where I now rest, sits in the south of Spain. I often linger on the spacious balcony, gazing across the Straits of Gibraltar and imagining how the Colossus of Rhodes might look standing astride the blue water. The waterfront home is palatial and furnished with antiques. I spend my days shopping for rare items to impart my own personal touch to the home.

Yes, my fortunes have changed for the better. I have everything I want. If I think of something I desire, it is only a moment's work to buy it or order it delivered. When the little whisper of doubt enters my mind, insisting something is not quite right, I thrust it away.

It's strange, but I swear I hardly remember the wedding. Maybe the head injuries damaged my memory or someone drugged me.

The tinkle of glass brings a careful smile to my face because I know my husband is preparing before-dinner drinks. He takes such care, always uses the exact amount of ice I like and garnishes my glass with a little surprise. Sometimes a flower fresh from the extensive gardens behind the house or perhaps a piece of aromatic, seasonal fruit. One evening, he handed me a wine glass with an extravagant diamond bracelet wrapped around the stem.

Could a marriage be more perfect? I try to believe that's true.

I admit it took some time for him to convince me. I'd never felt eager to bind myself to one man like some women, to assume a subservient role and lose my identity. In the end, his constant care and consideration of my feelings persuaded me otherwise.

Do I love him? I'd rather not answer.

The French doors opened and footsteps sound behind me. My mouth curves into a pseudo-smile as I feel a soft kiss brush the top of my head.

"Good evening, my dear. How was your day?" He settles into a chair beside me, handing me a glass filled with wine and fruit. "Do try the berries. I had them flown in this morning from California, especially for you."

"Thank you. Ah, yes, quite lovely. Perfect." I sniff the fragrant concoction. Fruity, sweet and yet a hint of tartness.

"Now, is there anything you need or want? Anywhere you'd like to go? I made quite a profit in sales this month." He beams, the over-indulgent husband, catering to my every whim.

"I'd like to know what business makes such a tidy profit."

He clenches his jaw muscles, just the tiniest bit. "My dear, you know I prefer to keep my business separate from my personal life. I've told you this already."

Why does a man refuse to tell his wife anything about his livelihood? It seems so strange to me. My parents shared everything with each other. How can a marriage survive with secrets? "Yes, you have. Please forgive me."

"Of course, my dear. As always, your wish is my command." My husband, Judge Beecher T. Oldham, smiles at me before leaning back in his chair to gaze at the ocean.

Only once, right now, will I admit this...

I lost when the heavens fell.